BLUE ON BLUE

QUENTIN S. CRISP was born in 1972, in North Devon, U.K. He studied Japanese at Durham University and graduated in 2000. He has had fiction published by Tartarus Press, PS Publishing, Eibonvale Press and others. He currently resides in Bexleyheath, and is editor for Chômu Press.

JACK RAGLIN has published articles on Enoch Bolles and the Golden Age of Illustration and is completing a book on the life and art of Enoch Bolles.

Quentin S. Crisp

Blue on Blue

With an Afterword by

Jack Raglin

for Chris Askew

Contents

Blue on Blue

I: Overture

IAM a citizen of the ASAF, the Alternative States of the American Fifties[1]. Many wonderful things have already been accomplished here, but wonder seems to find its level beneath our shoes, and we walk on it, and forget about it, and begin to complain of sore feet. We forget even that we are living in the Alternative States of the American Fifties, forget that it used to be called the USAF, the Unbelievable States of the American Fifties. But somehow I've stayed interested in the fribbles and flurries that are ignored though undeniable at the origins

---

1. The Alternative States of the American Fifties is an artificial history zone 'reclaimed' from sunken parallel time, a sanctuary-loop colonised by those who wished to reject certain ontological time switches by which the original American Fifties receded into the relative past of mainstream history. There are a number of different 'settings', or what might be called 'premises' (using the word in its novelistic sense), to the ASAF than to the culture and society of the mainstream American Fifties. In the history of the ASAF, that is to say, in its 'settings' (rather than in its genesis within mainstream history), Noah Webster never existed; other things in its composition are different to mainstream history, too.

and borders of the ASAF. Because of such interests in my life, now that I am poised on a cliff edge, I am reminded of edges and borders generally, and it occurs to me that this testament may be read outside of the ASAF—wonder, after all, implies elsewhere—and therefore I will try to keep universality in mind as I write, and not assume knowledge on the reader's part. This may help me in many ways. Since I am about to be swept, the mindfulness of universality may go some way to ensuring an exhilarating sweep.

My name is Victor Winton; I am a—largely unsuccessful—cartoonist and animator. I used to think—with my head only, and understanding little—that my favourite colour was green. Now I know it to be blue, and can't believe I will ever again deviate from something so deeply known. Well, it's no use explaining blue, but some out there may already know all that my invocation of blue implies, and others, after reading this, may come to know. Green may be eerie and slimy, and there may even be less green on our planet than blue, but blue is nonetheless more otherworldly. Food is green; pills are blue. Emeralds are rare; sapphires are incomparable. A bower is shelter; a waterfall is a blessing and a portal. Leaf against sky, fever against dream—the dreadful lurking octopus and the unthinkable swift sea-snake.

There are blues for all seasons and situations, but it is especially the blue of autumn that I love. As evening declines towards twilight, the soft blue air becomes as endlessly layered in its silence as steady rain. Blue on blue—a veil of tears, then one of hope, then tears again, with the mystery of depth distilling of this a clarity that yet gives no indication of what might form the final veil. Nonetheless, walking down an avenue where trees shed leaves on the paving, a heart and an eye trained to such things may perceive in this melancholy and most-French of blues also the gleaming blue of superimposition—blue-screen, they call it. Out of the blue, and onto the blue—the imagination finds this surely the most fertile of all aethers.

No doubt you'll hear everything I have to say about blue again, from me or those like the semi-mystic child-artists of Magic Daoism, who identify blue as the colour of special truth. It will be repeated. It doesn't matter; blue is inexhaustible.

In some part of me, I have always known about the nature of blue, but it is only surprisingly recently—and it's surprisingly difficult to be sure of this—that I have been truly conscious of the significance of blue in my own life and in the world I inhabit.

I think something quickened in the matrix of my understanding of blue in the springtime a year ago. (I love autumn, but it is spring with which this story begins and ends.) As winter evolved through its own mastery of things to uncertainty and gradually yielded its grip on street corners and the forefronts of people's attention to the stranger sunlight that the fickle world now demanded, I found myself forging the new habit of almost daily visits to the Brookdale Municipal Museum. A particular book had galvanised and directed me in the circuit of this routine, and the book and the Museum together had something—I'm sure—to do with the stirring up of my relationship with blue into a more urgent fascination. Not that either book or Museum were conspicuously blue; the truth is, both of them, though having the attractions of gravity, were as grey to me as the cracked surface of a dead planet.

Here is a typical passage from the book, *Universal Symbolism in Art*, by Aadharsh Ratnasingham:

> Do the planets seek out new directions? They may be dubbed 'wanderers,' but like Odysseus, their wanderings always come full circle. In the ancient world, the cyclical nature of all things was honoured. To modern eyes, the fatalism of the stoic—the true philosopher—appears sombre. We associate the past with oppression and widespread poverty, and believe stoicism a mere symptom of such social ills. In fact, the fatalistic spirit maintained an order like that of the cyclical heavens. Within such order, the wise citizen, subject, or even slave—such as that noble philosopher, Epictetus—could understand his relation to eternity, and anchor his soul within it, as the planets are anchored in their orbits to the blazing stars. What need have they for mere novelty when they have cosmos? It is in losing our orbit that we seek 'a better world.' We plummet like a comet, and since there is, in our newly relativistic

universe, neither up nor down, we blind ourselves to unsustainable contradictions, and decree that whatever way we are headed it is up; just so long as it is a straight line we call it 'progress,' never mind that we are on a collision course for catastrophe. In the meantime we congratulate ourselves on our freedom, which apparently only increases as we become ever more lost, ever farther from our cosmic home. In the arts, what this has meant is self-expression—something that avails us little when we are less and less able to believe that the self also implies a soul, with all a soul's responsibilities.

And so on.

The basic thesis of the book is that the function of art is to connect temporal humankind to eternity. This is effected through the understanding and application of sacred and immutable symbols—necessarily immutable since they are eternity's servants. Modern artists, the author contends, turning their back on eternity and facing towards individualism, are actually turning away from art itself into mere flimflammery, confusion and self-defeat. Perhaps the author would appreciate that, for me, all this brings to mind something from that "ancient world" of his: Scylla and Charybdis.

I could have tried asking his opinion, since he is an employee of the very Municipal Museum that I was beginning to frequent. But I'm sure he'd already made his opinion on all things as clear as possible in the book, and, even supposing a desire on my part that someone relieve me of the burden of thinking for myself, I don't think it would ever be long before I was confronted with something in life that the thoughts prepared for me did not and could not adequately address.

Lest I sound too wry, the volume of Dr. Ratnasing-ham impressed me in such a way that it not only marked my thoughts, but gave me momentum. Wasn't it my duty as an artist to come to the Museum and to study the universal symbols as manifest in the various and particular artefacts? In this way my work might acquire substance and weight almost pendulous enough that you could cup it in the palm of your hand. The good doctor's book induced in me this quasi-tactile enthusiasm, and bounced me into the lair of statuary archetypes. I had barely considered it, turning those pages, but very soon after I had stepped into the high-ceilinged chambers of the Museum it became obvious to me just what 'forms,' 'archetypes' and 'eidolons' meant. All Dr. Ratnasingham's talk of planets was not accidental; it contained a significance in which I now felt myself initiated. For the secret knowledge—so I thought—was, after all, not so very much more secret than innuendo. I was satisfied to realise I had come here to study with sketch-pad and pencil, goddesses. Of Plato's forms, the female was the most perfect. These were the greatest archetypes of all. The orbit of planets I saw in breast and behind, and well understood how their movements might command cosmic destiny. Was the music of the spheres, I pondered, no more than a wolf-whistle? In any case, it's true that the centre of erotic gravity on any comic book cover is the female figure. Beside this archetype, all others begin to pale to abstraction. And yet it is an archetype that retains an invincible strangeness, since who can say what it means and why it attracts?

Some days—for instance, when I was otherwise cooped up in an inky, creaking, gloom-panelled office, struggling with wrist-ache and the numbing flush of tedium—I would take my lunch in a brown paper bag— sturdy, with the mouth tidily roll-folded—to Crommessie Park, which was near enough to make the walk pleasant, and whose lawns were as refreshing in their green as a fountain in its burble. There I would locate a vacant bench and make quick work of my comestibles, a mite disappointed I had not tasted more, but pleased still to have time enough for an absorbing museum visit. In a way it was the sense of expansion that came before the concentration I anticipated that was the best part of the day, though it was composed of potentiality rather than fulfilment. The nation, of necessity, finds occasions to celebrate itself, but these are reminders of daily scenes, daily strivings, daily forms of repose, that are the celebrations' essence. To the Museum, I would step through streets that seemed a combination of the celebration and the celebrated—walk aware of each step, as if I were a tap dancer, my patent leather shoes a reminder of the glories of industry and commerce, castanetting against paving stones, which brought to mind that whatever streets were paved with, the very fact of paving meant civilisation, and therefore all streets paved are paved as with clouds.

Paving, however, was almost the least of it. I walked an intricate paradise displaying the regularity of a cut jewel. Its angels were those of glazing, masonry, steel-working, carpentry, hydraulics, electrical engineering, mail delivery, telegraph poles, printing presses, and so on; a here-and-there chimney-potted paradise engraved and varnished and bevelled, fluted, prinked and scrolled, and finished with finical finials. Even aware of my finite stock of allotted minutes, I would persuade myself that enchantment had some literal power to render time elastic, and would stop, here before the miracle of a milliner's window display, where hats sat like birds-of-paradise upon the perches of an aviary, and there—before a bakery where warm aromas made known directly to the olfactory sense a common, wordless, unanswerable affirmation of being, and where glazed pastry and frosting represented sweetness-for-its-own-sake to the eyes.

And then, as I approached nearer the region of the Museum, the streets would become more crowded with uniforms and fashions, and especially in the traffic, the wonders of the ASAF would become more explicit: vir-tuosos of the pogo-stick would demonstrate the loop-holes and limitations in gravity's law by soaring over heads to veer and swerve and pick through the moving weave of bodies; others with kite-umbrellas steered in a higher stratum of air, like colourful dandelion seeds; yet others glided sedate in the hanging baskets of balloons. All this unmistakably served—apart from any immediate, practical ends—to keep awake the stir and excitement of knowing this town, like many others throughout the ASAF, was a centre of wonders, though there have sometimes been complaints that individual aviation now constitutes a traffic that half-obliterates, for the simple pedestrian, the periwinkle sky that should be our first and enduring source of wonder.

But turning eyes earthward again can also be rewarding. First person experience should be—don't you think?—the highest level of fame possible, but in a rather ordinary, occasionally delightful way, it is actually the greatest obscurity, in which all things, though the epitome of real, seem to go entirely unrecorded. To notice these things—personal observation—can be fascinating, amusing, astounding, can induce emotions that no other person has words for, to bring them to wider consciousness. For instance, an occasion now rises in my mind on the cresting wave of memory: a woman—let us say 'lady,' since her figure, naturally or *un*, was in the corseted style that might suggest to some to address her, "Lady"—probably in her mid-twenties, with a blue hairband, hair as red as the deer of pristine forests, a white, one-piece dress, stockinged legs, was walking towards me. Behind her, a suited man tapped a white cane on the sidewalk. Glasses concealed his eyes, but the position of his head on his neck gave the odd impression, not of blindness, but of a fixed and focused gaze. The lady stopped and took something from her bag; the man stopped behind her. She turned, something of the double-take in her motion, then with determined stride and shoulders set, marched towards him, raising her hand… He flinched. The moment he flinched, his disguise was seen through from her side as from his; a primrose-gloved pinkness slapped his face hard. Clutching his jaw, he almost fell to the ground. The lady huffed, and departed.

X-ray spectacles have given rise to many such scenes as this. No legislation has been passed against them, but to be known to wear them in public can be a socially crippling thing. Some very clearly consider the social sacrifice worth the gains. Some—I hear it said and believe—enjoy being slapped most of all.

Such are the streets of Brookdale, the town in which I live. In those days of earliest spring, one year past, I would climb the wide, tiered steps of stone to the Museum, pigeons flapping from my feet, and everything would seem a delicious but unsatisfying overture; looked back upon it seems instead life's penultimate fullness, with the ultimate perhaps yet before me.

Arrived at the Museum entrance, I would pass through into its dignified gloom like an actor—perhaps not a great one—taking the stage. I would feel myself glide between the massy columns of the grand interior, and I would find a harbour in which to dock myself where I could, without trouble, take out my sketch-pad and play 'pavement artist' to the female deities of that curatorial cosmopolis in which Olympus merged with Valhalla. I would spend twenty or so minutes at anchor, reconstructing, according to such principles of art as I was equipped with, dancing Kali's world-shaking thighs, or attempting to re-conjure from the spell of oils on canvas, the tragic muliebrity of lovely, flame-tressed Brynhild, the Valkyrie. Artistically, I considered—or tried to consider—the Museum as something combining a gymnasium, an academy and a temple. I hoped that my visits were serving to develop artistic muscle, philosophy, and that relationship *between* and transcendence *of* muscle and philosophy that is—soul. Or, to put it in terms perhaps more fitting, that is *daimon*.

On days other than office days, I was able—and most willing—to spend greater time there. Among the many things picked up in my studies was this, from Pindar:

> Neither by ship nor on foot would you find
> The marvellous road to the assembly of the
> Hyperboreans.

If the only study worth devoting mortal hours to is how to find one's passage to Hyperborea, on the occasions I had more time, I often broke through, after pains, to something like an absorbing, effortless concentration within whose circle I felt I was making progress indeed towards my Hyperborean goal. Certainly, movement had occurred; I had moved, but Hyperborea, it seemed, was no nearer.

On days such as this, my appetite for dream and beauty half-sated, half-frustrated, when I put away my sketch-pad, I would not go straight home, but would haunt awhile the adjacent Sea Monkey Kingdom, which, more brightly illuminated than the Museum, and livelier with voices, to me had come to seem, compared with

the Museum, a kingdom of shadows. Nonetheless, I lingered solo about its dazzle-fronded, stalagmited, artificial
grottoes, eavesdropped on the eerie amphibious beauty
of the sea monkey songs, even watched some of the
aquabatics, like someone who had no business there.
Actually, I feel I have had some hand—anonymously—
in the existence of Sea Monkey Kingdom. I was not the
first, but as a young man, frantic for any kind of work in
the world of comic books, I was one of the copywriters
who contributed prose (and more notably, verse) to the
adverts in comic books for sea monkey pets. At the time,
though I really knew nothing of sea monkeys, I even
told myself that what I wrote was a kind of phantastic
poetry.

Sea Monkeys!

Watch them spook and play,
In their merry, mellow-ghoulish, slime-green
    jelly way,
Their gibbous paws on bubbling lutes,
Their females sway in haunting hula,
Glib-hipped, loose-lipped, eerie and gay,
Their children splashing with hoops in pools—
What a hoot on the knobs of their kooky
    green horns!

These rapidly growing animalcula,
They'll trouble you with their undersea fun
Both day & night, night & day.

They're waiting for you in their watery castle.
Come and be friends with them!
Fill out the form! Send one dollar today!

The advert that used my copy was pulled soon after
its appearance in a handful of comic book titles, and replaced with one whose text accentuated the fun while
eliminating the eerie. I have heard of real people I've
never met asserting that the 'spooky' sea monkeys advert
that vanished so quickly has particular nostalgic value
for them. Unfortunately, I wrote it, so it's hard for me
to achieve the kind of detachment that would be a pre-
requisite for nostalgia in this case. Anyway, visiting Sea
Monkey Kingdom, seeing all the popular attractions, like
the Coronation of the Sea Monkey King, Sea Monkey
Honky Tonk Time, and the Web-Footed Chorus Line,
I came to be assailed by complex yet primal feelings it
seems indecent to describe. Privately, I have long referred
to Sea Monkey Kingdom as 'the Pensivarium.' Its com-
mercially cultivated image of otherworldly entertainment
and glad-rag, good-time magic has been skilfully calcu-
lated to eclipse the necessity on which it was founded—
thousands of unwanted sea monkey pets flushed into
the sewers by bored owners when those pets were still
babies.

And from the Museum and Sea Monkey Kingdom, I
would go home… to an uncarpeted apartment in which
the roof sloped unpeacefully over my bed—here in this
City of Wonders.

I did say that it was the book and the Museum that

re-enlivened my interest in blue. Between Museum and book, I was at that time so taken with the idea of serious and pioneering study that, as well as driving myself hard at the sketch-pad and easel, I also scrawled out a ream or two of inky notes in the best scholarly style I could muster. They—I suppose—are the lengthy harbingers of this briefer testament. I'll attempt a digest of their main points here, also giving some idea of what had been their external stimuli.

First of all, there was a day when I was wondering querulously how, in a world as wondrous as ours, people could still find it in themselves to thrill to the flimsy and childish delights of comic books, with their vicarious adventures and their cheap sexual titillation. Querulously, of course, because I was thinking myself on the sickening verge of obsolescence, which feels to a human's beating heart as daylight does to a ghost. Surely, I thought, now that wonder upon wonder has arrived, with the forecast on all channels being 'more wonder,' this not-so-respectable but colourful trade in escapism that I have loved so dearly, must soon evaporate? And surely it is selfish of me to wish for it to linger? In this mood, I visited a drug store that I knew to have a prominent display of comics, flapping at and sticking to the eyes like bats with bubble-gum wings. I asked there how they were selling. Briskly, it seemed. And an odd certainty grew on me that this particular candy-coloured brand of Scotch mist was not going to vanish in the sunlight of our bright, wakeful age—not just yet. Maybe not for a long time. But why?

Under the urging of this question, I examined those comic books with newly scholastic eyes. Many of the publishers whose wares were displayed were purveyors of horror—naturally—but it was not the obsolescence—or otherwise—of this branch of the industry that engaged my attention. The questions surrounding *that* theoretical obsolescence are slightly different to the questions that occupied me, and I will pass them over. A combination of two recurrent factors in what I saw began to tickle up inside me a mental archway with the geometry of insight about it. Those two factors were, first—this one no surprise—the eternally novel erotic tease of myriad femininity, and second, a sense of *nameless* fantasy. I say "nameless"—I will now attempt to describe it. It was a fantasy characterised especially by curves and by colours at once bright and pale—gay, fairground colours, in fact. The juxtaposition of pink and yellow particularly represented it, and it was notably given—but by no means limited—to vistas of undersea worlds; the future; the Far East; holiday resorts; the planet Venus; paradisiacal islands; combinations of these. The images were full of a lemon-and-strawberry optimism. They suggested a life where the sweetness of mystery is no longer a fugitive sensation at the edges of awareness, but permeates all things, inner and outer, in a perfect fusion of wispy syrup and zesty tang. The fantasy was nameless, I realised, because it belonged to anyone. Good or bad, in theory, no one was barred. The traditions of history were only reflected here in dream-like ways that dissolved the authority of their judgements, and so solemnity was absent. Without official sanction of any kind, this was the most personal of all heavens. There were no angels here. This was the heart's own nameless not-yet home, as young, otherworldly and all-comprehending as futurity itself.

Here a child with gold leaves in his hair sat astride a green and pink polka-dotted turtle which soared through the sherbet twinkles of some nebula beyond the range of Earth's telescopes; a quaint temple stood on the slopes of a mountain where flowers bloomed gigantically, its venerable roof-tiles coloured like a tray full of confectioner's treasure; girls with Alice bands in their hair rode inflatable animals through a flotilla of parasolled tables into a cosmic vortex of marbled genie-lamp smoke; and so on.

I should mention this 'nameless fantasy' was not always in a pure form, but often blended with the dream images of horror or other genres.

Remembering the sugar impact of excitement that had first attracted me to comics, I bought on the spot a selection of the most irresistible of the titles. (Or rather, of the covers, since it was really the covers that sold them.)

I took the comics home and, as it were, placing them on the testing tongue of my brain, spectro-analysed them. The mention of a tongue is appropriate. It seemed to me that all of the comics were designed—consciously or not—to stimulate a psychical saliva. They were, so to speak, appetisers, menus for possible worlds, for beautiful or thrilling experiences. But for there to be such a

trade in appetisers when the feast for which the appetite
was stimulated was either a) available elsewhere with no
need to purchase the appetisers, or b) available nowhere
within the bounds of current existence, was a curious
thing. It was while this observation intrigued me that I
noticed a recurring ink-tone used in conjunction with a
particular mode of feminine clothing. Here it was, used
for that garment that hangs like a veil before the loins of
an odalisque; there it was, too, used for the bikini of a
pale-skinned, winsome-kneed redhead on a beach towel;
and there again, in the negligée and half-visible underwear of a beribboned belle at her dressing mirror.

The following is a condensed version of some of the
notes I wrote as a consequence of this haphazard insight, which had come to me with the sense of distress
and liberation that might accompany the collapse of a
long-standing wall:

> Aquamarine—Since my recent impulse pur-
> chase of a half-random selection of com-
> ics, I have come to understand something
> about this colour. In order to compare, I
> sifted through my existing stock of comics
> and purchased more with research in mind.
> After extensive and varied experiments us-
> ing myself as the test subject, I have reached
> the conclusion that aquamarine is the ulti-
> mate erotic colour. Red is more commonly
> associated with the erotic, and any colour of
> underwear may superficially seem the most

erotic colour *in situ*, but aquamarine is the only colour that is erotic in the abstract, even when not rendered as underwear or seen in juxtaposition with human skin. The blue, by itself, would be too expansive, detached, or melancholy. The green tinge functions like a blush, stimulated by contraction. The tips of things can be concentrated areas of sensitivity. The vulva, for instance, seems to converge to a disappearing tip. This convergence and disappearance is a kind of contraction. From this contraction there is born shame, embarrassment, or something similar for which there is no common term. This, expanding again, becomes an intolerable quivering bliss. And this is aquamarine.

Aquamarine is a between colour—between blue and green—and this is a fact essential to the understanding of its nature. Let us analyse—or 'anal eyes'—the word 'between', by breaking it into its constituent parts:

'Be'—although a small word, this is wide in meaning—one might say 'broad'—and is obviously of a fleshly character.

'Tween'—this indicates division.

When conjoined in the word 'between,' these elements form a (w)hole that corresponds either to the vulva or the buttocks, both of which, in their respective ways, are divided 'being.'

From all of the preceding it becomes clear that aquamarine has the esoteric quality of a 'fairy fire.' And this is the precise function of an aquamarine bikini on the cover of a comic book—a fairy fire, a signal, a promise of something yet to come, a token of good faith from another world whose sweet portals are, at present, closed.

But what can it be—in a world such as ours—that is yet to come?

Another occasion for making notes began when I found myself dissatisfied with my new character sketches, the first in which I had tried to incorporate what I thought I had learned from the Museum. The characters I drew had swallowed the archetype-planets that had so impressed me, but not digested them, resulting in bulges like stolen goods. On an impulse, I took a colour plate I had of Disney's Snow White character design and laid it on my desk, next to a full-page photograph, in the *National Geographic*, of a Babylonian statue of Ishtar, the former with a bird on her finger, flanked by chipmunks, the latter bird-footed and flanked by owls. This is the kernel of what I wrote:

Ratnasingham would tell us that the modern Snow White is both derivative and rootless, emphasising the latter trait; in other words that it is a creation that is not nourished directly by its sources. Ratnasingham does not acknowledge the possibility of new sources for creativity, or even the idea that creativity might mean making something new, so whether a creation resembles old sources or not, the judgement is the same—it is a bad copy.

But this is arbitrary. One has to insist as an article of faith that the older forms are definitive to agree with this. Without such dogma, the argument ceases to be compelling. One might as well argue that right has precedent over left, white over black, hot over cold, as argue that old is necessarily better than new. If eternity is our ideal, then we must admit that to privilege the old over the new is to be preoccupied with the merely temporal. In fact, if time makes sense at all from the point of view of eternity, surely, it must be a teleological sense, implying a greater value in later things. I hesitate to assert this—in any case, it is far from a simple matter to substantiate the dogma that virtue belongs to the past.

To return to Snow White, the Disney version, no doubt, is laughable from the point of view of authenticity, her clothes a barely recognisable parody of their source. But their degree of unrecognisability is such that it contains an element of *sui generis* creation, and what can be more authentic than that?

The Disney Snow White is syrupy, populist, lacks substance? What, then, is the original folk tale, if not populist? What are fairy tales if not the very genius of sentiment? As for substance, we do not yet know which version of Snow White will last longest in time, but in terms of population, we can already calculate with confidence that the latter—chronologically speaking—covers the greater area. Let us be fair and speculate that one extends exactly as far in the dimension of width as the other does in the dimension of length. In our lives, does not the resonance of antiquity, as manifest in an ancient statue, meet its equal, at least, in the trivial, immediate resonance of the familiar, as manifest in the cartoon character? That which is near, though small, is as significant as that which is large, though far.

However, I suppose Ratnasingham would profess not to prefer the old to the new merely on principle, but because of the individualistic spirit which newer things tend to evince, and which he decries. This spirit correlates not so much with chronological newness as with novelty; it is novelty he opposes. In essence, individualism is a breaking faith with the universal; Ratnasingham implies that the individual, at least, is weakened by this division. Perhaps he fears that the universal is, too—that individualism is mere disintegration. Here is the riven and harrowed heart of the matter: by cleaving to the universal we maintain contact with eternity, but sacrifice plurality; by striking out on the path of individualism, we gain the infinite in plurality, but sacrifice eternity.

Snow White, in fact, has much in common with early goddess archetypes and could easily be just another iteration of them, but she also has about her a scent or an aura of novelty. My own artwork has something in common with this novelty. Ratnasingham execrates sentimentality—perhaps that's it. When I examined the lines of my artistic figures and fancies, there was about them—unfailingly—a wistfulness that could only be personal, a kind of moistness. But putting aside my own work, and putting aside wistfulness, this Snow White is like Santa Claus. It may appear that she is a bad copy, but that unfaithfulness to sources—which to some may even seem ignorance—clearly has its own genius. This cartoon Santa Claus, this cartoon Snow White—who can deny that they have penetrated the very depths of the human psyche?

And after writing the notes of which the above forms a précis, I was struck by my use of the word 'faith.' If faith is the virtue of the older forms of art, I had to acknowledge that I already had my own kind of faith— nameless, perhaps, but natural to me, and in that sense of greater authority than the merely temporally antique.

Newly inspired, I set about reaffirming the path of my own faith. I began work on sketches for another new character. After all, when I discarded thoughts of archetypes, I worked better. Maybe I was working with archetypes, anyway, but they were, for me, archetypes that were alive—therefore impossible to study—in a way that the older ones were not. I saw that my lines, when I did not try to follow principles, displayed their own natural, and therefore fuller—more elastic—principles. A cartoon character, after all, must live, and this requires the principle that transcends principles. A few lines on paper, a few supple curves—I was beginning to see a person here. A person with this willow-bend for a cheek-bone must have a certain kind of nose, fingers just so, and there is only a particular look in the eye that will do. And I must call her Lara, for that is her name, undoubt-edly. And this collection of lines coheres in its principle so well and so lovelily—Lara Lovelily, that's it—that if I have the skill to follow the principle as I should, a differ-ent collection of lines guided by the same principle, will be immediately recognisable as Lara from another angle, Lara in a different mood, Lara by moonlight, and so on.

But where do the lines come from, and where the principle with which they are forged? Yes, truly, this was something important—I was beginning to understand. That little book on Magic Daoism (*Volume II*)—that agreeable book that for some reason had been partially banned across the ASAF—on the twitchy urgings of intuition, I left the drawing desk, and the assorted fragments of Lara on various sheets of paper, and went over to my bookshelf, and slid one slim volume from between two thick, and opened and read at random:

> White is the colour of universals. Said to contain all colours, nonetheless it is symbolic of emptiness. The root meaning of the word 'blank' is 'white.' In some cultures this is explicitly the colour of death. In other cultures, it is indirectly the colour of death, since it represents the void of light from which all emerges and to which all returns. Black, as the colour of death, has a more melancholy aspect, essentially evoking incarceration in a lightless cell, but this has its comforts, which are personal and bodily. White, though a kind of liberation, is also ultimate loss. The root meaning of the word 'bleak' is also white.
>
> White is the old colour of truth, but to whom? No one's truth is white. Inspiration is not without flavour or tint. The colour of Magic Daoism is blue.

And I saw this blue clearly, existing independently of space and time, more real than both—pale blue like twilight on an avenue of trees in a French comic book. Pure blue. A deep bluescreen of the soul and the imagination, on which all beautiful and comforting things might be projected or from which they might—out of the blue—occur.

It was from this blue that my pencil lines came—that's why I had always known it. This blue was the principle that transcended principles. This was the taste, the wish, the Binah that understands[1], the dainty fingers of personality and the swirling fingerprint lines of individuality, this sigh that returns like a forgotten and indescribable scent that never dies but only you ever knew, this tingle between familiar and strange, this you that never there was word for, this identifiable but untransmittable sensation, this atmosphere without reason, this illicit fairy kiss for which you are more fool than sinner, this only thing that God and Satan mistakenly left you for your own and which both (and everyone else besides) insist to you is worthless—this, your only and invisible, your peculiar—this secret blue.

---

1. It's possible that Victor Winton is confused here in his Qabbalah scholarship. Traditionally, the colour associated with Binah is green. Blue is the colour of Chokhmah, which corresponds to 'wisdom', and stands as the first interface between Keter and the remaining sephirot.

II: Buena Vista

ND it was with this blue epiphany that Lara first
came to me. She was its herald, and then she was
its cargo. I did not realise it then, but in this first coming there was a mermaid imperfection to her form, or
its principle, or my grasp of its principle. Lara Lovelily.
I think of that prototype with a retrospective fondness
that, because of her blemishes, threatens to overflow into
something unbearable. Still, I know she is of the past.

But at the time...

My awareness was shaped by the winds of other sensations than now. Let me recall how, at home, I sat at my
literal drawing board, the sun rising as if from within the
clean void of paper before me, and how the lines of the
telegraph wires outside my window would reassure me
that there was order in the world—others were doing
their work and I must do mine. They provided the lines
on which I must write the notes of my melody. Yes, and
as the birds warbled on those wires, I understood there
was no need to whistle while I worked when my work

was to whistle. Dutiful and fresh came the songs of the sparrows; dutiful and fresh the woodpecker chisel and peck, the dot and the dash, of the sharpened lead of my pencil. Those eyes soft as primrose, bright as sunlight caught in amber, those cheeks rounded by the rays of days and nights when swallow-tailed men and bow-bustled women spoke of hearts and knew of what they spoke, those lips ever moist with tender readiness for the innocent exclamation, "Why!" What was their darling melody? I will write of that later.

The sun rose higher, on office days calling me to less canorous industry. When it descended again, often I would be at the same drawing board, the mellowing light framing my vision of the work at which my hand flicked and drooped with an appropriate haze of sepia and gold.

Although my pencillurgy, where educated, was more of the school of subtlety and softness, my lines willowy and my shading downy, there was an unprecedented rightness to my sketches of Lara that spruced her fluffy chignon into something brash as the blast from a steam train's whistle. This rightness—healthy, cheerful, not without sauce—gave the work momentum, and persuaded me that I had struck here onto the true path of my talent. Lara Lovelily would be the incarnation—or the inscribation—of that female charisma I knew in my heart but could not, myself, live. A girl—no, a veritable gal—of beguiling quirks like skilful cosmetics, she would fizz with novelty, but, free of the slightest maculation of awkwardness, would clack her sassy red high heels right into that chamber of the collective bosom that has "we've been waiting for you, friend" written home-sweet-homely over the lintel.

I suffered, however, with the frustration that comes from planning, and being in the early stages of, something great. The greatness is wide—expansive as a sky full of fireworks—but the way to it is narrow and logjammed. I'm sure it must have been said there are no shortcuts to greatness. Perhaps it would be more appropriate to say, "no shortcuts to reality." Perhaps it is merely the same thing. So I fretted over the nuances of a knee bone, wishing that my pencil was not forced to the insect crawl of details in the pursuit—how can one crawl in pursuit?—of a vision that continued to race even as I contemplated. How stupendous would be the adventures of Lara Lovelily, even at their most inconsequential, how extradimensional her style, so that charm and whimsy would combine with the force of sorcery to bring to minds simple, sophisticated or staid a caressing sensation of genial zephyrs from alien worlds. With no need for intellectuality, the understanding of the reader would be dilated. Lara would merely hitch a stocking top, or recline twinkling upon a diving board, and the cosmos would drip the golden honey of prolific interconnection, and portals would open that had been aeon-closed between love and actualisation, and through them would cluster a traffic of mellow lightning.

On a day that was not an office day, I finished a finely shaded drawing of Lara in a bathing suit, and, taking care to draw only in the restrained overflowing of plenitude, and having an eye-that-knows-what-it-wants attentive to the correspondence between the rainbow-implications of this smile-bunched cheek and this gluteal curve, I found I had arrived at something that almost could be called 'fully formed.' And so I laid down my pencil and wondered—the agony of wonder—how long it would require to move from *almost* to *entirely*, and how long then before I might take that completed form dancing through the adventures for which she was made.

I decided then to distract myself from my impatience with a cigarette and a newspaper. My current office work would not last much longer. With my energies engaged in projects—such as Lara—still very much speculative, I had, even at my untender, though yet untoughened age, not achieved the reassuring stability of a job with prospects.

I went out, bought the daily paper from a newsstand, and took it to a diner, to read with a fresh, black coffee. Spreading the printed sheets upon the table top was like breaking the crust of a newly baked loaf. I smoothed the surface of the paper perhaps more than was necessary. A newspaper is basically a map of the present—not necessarily a good map, but even what is selected (and by implication what excluded) can be informative. Sometimes we may feel chastened by what we read, finding that we have wandered from the main street of human affairs. But there is more to life than main streets, and front and back are relative terms.

On the front page of the *Brookdale Examiner* (the number for Tuesday, March the 3rd, 1957i), surrounding a photograph so spectacular it was almost three-dimensional, was an in-depth and somewhat breathless (albeit in a clipped, journalistic way) story concerning the final unveiling, after a miraculous nine years of construction, of the Buena Vista Castle, to the northwest of the city. The way the towers of the castle seemed to lean and swell towards the camera, I guessed the photograph had been taken from the giddy basket of a hot air balloon. The headline ran:

Buena Vista—As Close As You Get

The story was intriguing to me in many of its details, inflating within me that energetic fascination that brings one alive to the world in general, with a desire to engage, to understand, to be implicated in, to make new. But this is not the most appropriate place in my account of things to write at length about Buena Vista Castle. That lucid-dream edifice figures later in the events whose reality and meaning I am attempting to chart. I might avail myself of the opportunity then to lay out for examination the facts—as I grasp them—which are the setting for a building that glows lunar with the reflected light of all our dreams.

On the third page of that newspaper was something that interested me in a very different way. Nothing else among the stories of the day at once so consternated me through the forced reacquaintance with my helplessness among the crowding developments of the universe, and so intoxicated me with a sense that if things must titanically change then I may freely, and at my own risk, meddle with the instruments of change before all is fixed, the change done, and the instruments are safely put away. It was a one-column story constituting the latest in a series of irregular updates on the progress made by Dr. Ingram and his team in the perfection of a teleportation machine. According to the information presented there, tests with living subjects had reached such a stage that the doctor and his colleagues could realistically expect to teleport the first human, *without the need to travel in intervening space*, from one terminal to another, within a year.

At the foot of the article, giving the impression of collaboration between the newspaper and the team whose project they were reporting, was a note directing the reader to a full-page advert elsewhere within the same issue. The advert, in sixteen-point letters, was as follows:

> Have you been waiting for a chance to prove yourself? Does the world feel too small for the great things you believe you can do? This could be your opportunity.
>
> As you will have read, Dr. Ingram and his team have succeeded in the impossible—the teleportation of both inanimate objects and living beings from one location to another almost instantaneously. Now they invite you to become part of their success. Within a year, preparations will have been completed for the teleportation of the first human

being. In a historic project of this nature, all possible precautions are observed, and the greatest capacity of human resources in expertise, thoroughness, intelligence and moral purpose are brought to bear. The first human trial will, under no circumstances, proceed before the project organisers are 100 per cent certain that no physical or mental danger can befall the subjects. Nonetheless, to be the first to step over such a momentous threshold is an act of heroism that must be honoured, and we intend to ensure that all those taking part in the first human trials receive the honours they deserve.

Etc. Etc.

Among what followed, the salient information was that 100 human trial subjects would be selected from forthcoming volunteers, that there would be a cash prize for all selected, and that, in addition, these first 100 teleported humans would receive a certificate testifying such, and would have their names engraved in a specially commissioned monument to memorialise this epoch-making etc.

The advert ended with an address to write to for further information and volunteer application forms.

For a moment I saw the name 'Victor Winton' engraved somewhere in a solemn, silent roll call of 100 names. To be finalised like that—not merely in 'black and white,' but in bronze and marble—would be a relief (despite being an intaglio). No further effort would be required. I would be an enduring name, and nothing more, without hunger, without sensation, without weakness—an ideal.

Memorialised—the word came back to me, prompting me to re-read the advert. In fact, the words 'monument' and 'commemorate' had been used, but there was no 'memorial' or any of its immediate cognates. This, in turn, prompted me to re-read the article from which I had been referred to the advert. It contained answers that Dr. Ingram had made to a number of questions.

> "You could say it's the safest form of travel, provided the initial information has been correctly recorded by the hydragraph. In a sense, it's not really travel at all. It's communication—rapid communication. And if the source retains the original message, it can be re-sent in the case of miscommunication. In essence, one teleportation terminal is communicating the memory of an object, a creature, or—in the near future—a human being to another terminal, which recreates the original from this perfect memory."
>
> "So the actual object does not travel at all?"
>
> "As I said, it's very safe. Naturally, because of complications that might arise otherwise, the original must always be absorbed. Essentially, the original becomes

the spare—a shed skin, if you like—and the energy of its absorption is stored to power future teleportation."

It had been a long time since my thoughts had hovered in such uncertainty. Then, as if this act itself were a commitment, I took the fountain pen from my breast pocket and circled the address at the bottom of the advert.

Reading the article and the advert left me with—among other things—the feeling of being in competition with something vast. How can a comic book artist and animator be in competition with a team of scientists and technicians developing a teleport system? And yet that was distinctly and unfadingly how I felt. Was it the idea of being replaced—implied in the article—that had given rise to this feeling? Or was it that same sense I had been preoccupied with before, of imaginary wonder competing with actual wonder, now made keen again by the proximity of something that might entirely destroy one of the four walls comprising the comfortable room 'normality'? Perhaps the answer was yes in both cases. It also came to me that I had been considering recently—if ever so vaguely—my comic book work as a wonder that might cross the boundary from imaginary to actual, and in that sense I was competing with the wonders of the world around me as I had not been before. 'Vaguely' is all very well until it is pointed out. My aspirations—or at least my means of realising them—now seemed puny. Yet what was puny—even starved—consistently failed to die. Ghosts, perhaps, need little sustenance.

Despite my sense of disaffection with Ratnasingham's universal symbols and their fixed orbits, a fresh determination to possess their secrets surged within me—no doubt because of that edition of the *Brookdale Examiner*—and my cardiovascular system pumped oxygen and blood through my limbs with the tang of diligence and discipline as I strode up the Museum steps in the following days.

What unexpected, waited-for thing would harmonise a solitary life with the wonderful world in which it goes about its business? What could prime the heart for firing? What, in establishing connections and correspondences between the multiplicitous nodes of existence, could make those nodes effloresce unimaginably so that a cascading superabundance of dimensions never mentioned outside of the experience of them is folded uncontainably into the otherwise deficient though persuasively real three?

I did not know, of course, that a trap awaited me, as I tapped more on toes than heels up those stone steps. I could not have suspected the nature of the trap—wonderful, heart-rending and many other things—when first it sprang, though I believed, when it did, that I had known all along, and next believed in despair that I had known all along I was wrong when I had thought I'd known all along. It has been a trap of multiple phases, reverses and unforeseeable developments. At times I have thought, wretchedly, that I am out of the trap at last; at other times I have realised with a sensation of the queerness of destiny that I am still in it. As I write this, I am sure I am still in it—sure with only a tiny, sickening doubt to crack the sureness. I anticipate that the phases of the trap will further unfold, beyond my anticipation of them. On the other hand, I feel I comprehend the trap entirely now and that therefore the final phase is before me.

But I will try to forget the layers of knowing and unknowing that have accumulated in time, and return to the present as it existed prior to the springing of the trap, a present which destiny ensured I play as if it were the very outpost of uncertainty.

Somehow, shortly after entering the Museum on the die-casting occasion of which I am thinking, I took a turning into a room I had not visited before, which was then the site of a temporary exhibition—on loan from another museum—of artefacts from Antient Quanzipuck. Well lit and almost central among the various exhibits was an eight-foot statue of the sea monkey deity, Zwila, goddess of ebb tides, postnatal depletion, forgetfulness and plentiful spawning, whose emblem was the sunken ship (tomb to sailors and lair to sea creatures). The tuberculated digits of her right paw assumed the 'dead crab' gesture in mystical recognition of the vacancy of completed forms, and in her left paw she held a twangtenna, like an amalgam of shepherdess's crook, sceptre and Jew's harp. This room, far from all exterior walls, was windowless, so that there was only artificial light to rescue it from gloom. I suppose the statue was not designed for such light; it looked unreal, and—maybe therefore—enchanted. In a room that was a cornucopia of the Quanzipuckian mythical imagination, replete with whelk curves and shrimp serifs, the statue of Zwila magnetised my imagination, like a living dream. Even so, the statue was soon supplanted in my awareness by the figure standing in front of it.

She had her back to me so that I saw her in less than quarter-profile. She was no one I knew and I looked at her initially with that indifference that is normal in our feelings towards an unfamiliar person. I think I first noticed—that is, my indifference ceased when I saw—her stockinged calves, appearing electrically vivid below the hem of her skirt. Her blouse, with puffs of pastry-pinching at the shoulders, was neat in cut, delicate in material, daintily white in hue. She looked as if she were, like me, on her lunch break. Her attire had the primness of the office about it, but with trimmings that prettily suggested the freckled soul of a person, as sensitive, private and natural as flesh is, beneath.

Those vivid stockings, with her red high heels and her Venus-in-clamshell foam of auburn hair, caught the same light in which the statue of Zwila seemed so pliably ready to raise her hand to cover a yawn. She was, as it were, highlighted. And it was when the various elements of her figure were assimilated by me into a highlighted whole, that a thrill ran through me, wobbling my stomach and other parts sensitive to such currents, and I told myself—mentally pounding a well-I-never fist in the palm of a hand—that, "I know this girl!" (experiencing

the urge to style it "this gal"), but then, in the backrush
of that very thrill, wobbling again with, "Of course I
don't," but not dissuading myself sufficiently of this to
return—unbelieving—to indifference.

In that state of suspension, I veritably hovered towards her, though some prickling aura prevented me
all of a sudden from hovering right to her side, and my
course changed so that I found myself examining the
statue with a gaze parallel to hers, and a respectable—
though barely—distance between my position and hers
at the guard rail. Like something I'd just thought of—
though I was hardly thinking—I took my sketchpad from
my briefcase and began to sketch. By now I could see
more of the girl's profile. There must have been some
ambiguity as to whether I was sketching her or the statue,
and I played on this. She was curious enough or unsettled
enough that she cast quick glances in my direction—her
left. I suspected she was lingering in front of this statue
longer than she might have otherwise in order to see what
I drew, or else in the suspicion that she was, in fact, posing for me. I responded to her glances perhaps slightly
more confidently, perhaps slightly more nervously, than I
would have without the ploy I had adopted of producing
my sketchpad, and the strange energy of (surely false)
recognition. I looked away with calm deliberateness, or I
smiled. Her hair had been—from behind—what almost
clinched things, though it was worn in a different style.
When she looked my way, however, my blood acceler-
ated within me, and all thought was thrown back in its
saddle by the force.

Sketchpad and pencil were harness and reins to me. The second nature established by long training kept me on my metaphorical mount. Is there a difference between control and command? I felt less of the former, more of the latter, and the results on paper surpassed what I would usually have intended. This moment was a shoot from a rhizome whose unseen roots spread deep and wide—I felt this, and almost gambled on tearing the finished sketch from my pad and presenting it to the subject with the single word, "Lara!" as if both addressing her and explaining the gift I offered. I think, in the end, I would not have done so. I can't be sure of what would have happened, because the girl herself intervened, thus furnishing an easier means of bridging the strangeness between us, of which I availed myself.

"What are you drawing?" she asked.

"I come here," I said, "to sketch goddesses."

And the flourish with which I then passed her the torn-out sheet served to underline and to distract from my meaning, as if with scrolling curlicues.

She took the sheet from me—a gesture establishing a treaty for small talk. What did her eyes see on that paper? I think that something impressed her, and something puzzled her. What I saw, for the first time, now that I did not have to avert my eyes strategically, was that this girl was not Lara. She was close, and I was impressed, too, even in my disappointment, but a new theme began to emerge among my varying sensations: It was a jarring tingle that seemed attached to the pinkness of this girl's skin, to the simultaneous difference from and similarity to Lara in the outline of her poodle curls, and to the soul-freckles and sensitivity I had been aware of from the first, but which now were developed into a particular otherness of which my expectations had been merely one momentary shadow-shape. And yet, without those false expectations, I would not have won my way into this harbour of engagement in the port of this fresh, unknown life.

Disappointment was detachment; it was also fascination. That jarring tingle moved through this trinity of feelings and I studied in the way that one does when no longer sure even of the existence of one's own studying soul.

Her eyes certainly could see, but they were not the blue of Lara's eyes; they were paler, shallower, oddly tinged with green, and seemed to tremble. Her forehead was perhaps narrower, her jaw a touch sharper, but it was especially this I noticed: her lips. They were definitely wrong. It almost vexed me. They were soft, complicated lips. What was it about them? Then I had it—they had been crossed out. Misdrawn and crossed out.

She extended her hand to pass the sheet of paper back to me.

My inner concept of Lara had provided the armature for the sketch, so that I had really not needed to scrutinise this girl too egregiously. Perhaps this had also been in my favour. But…

"Well, it's very flattering," she said.

"Oh, please keep it."

Although probably it was my finest portrait of Lara to date.

"I couldn't."

"It's yours. Really."

"That's very kind of you. I'm afraid I have nothing to carry it in."

My movements as I drew out some materials from my briefcase and improvised a protective envelope for the sketch were a little fussy, a little fumbly, but not too much; delayed assurance slowly percolated through them into steadiness.

"And you should sign it."

I nodded, adding a scribble to the corner of the sketch at which she squinted.

"Victor Winton," I said, to clarify.

"Do I know that name?"

"I'd be surprised. I have worked on the hand drawing for some of the big studios' animated features, but I'm only one of many. You won't see our names in the titles."

"Maybe someday."

To words of hope, there is no answer—especially sympathetic hope. I might have let this hope defeat me. The beginnings of the motion that would be turning away and leaving were already winding their springs up inside me. But gracelessly I snatched at a chance the moment I felt myself snagged on it.

"I still don't know your name."

"It's Jenny Mills."

Plain as the name of a shop girl, but that jarring tingle surged icily at the sound of it. The blade of otherness, perhaps, slicing into me with the sharpness of the ordinary.

"There's a diner, just by Crommessie Park, called Millie's. Do you know it?"

"I do. I go there sometimes."

"Perhaps you'd have time for a cup of coffee, before you go back to work?"

"Oh, I'm not going to work today. Actually, I'm looking for work."

We had entered a conversation, and seemed to obey now the conversation's will. Perhaps ten minutes later, I was looking down at the paving stones where my shoes and hers stepped leisurely forward, as if rolling the world beneath us, and thinking… not how natural it all seemed, but how secure a reality despite its unnaturalness, and how this unnaturalness was uncomfortable only to the degree of an optimally pleasing self-consciousness. Jenny—I learnt—had been interviewed for secretarial work that morning at an office not far from the Museum. Having nothing to do with the rest of her day, and feeling somewhat lackadaisical after the emotional pressure of the interview, she had, almost without deciding to, ended up diverting herself from all her current preoccupations by aimlessly wandering through the Museum's various exhibits. For me it was an office day, but I found myself unable to tell Jenny this; it was necessary that she believe I had, by happy chance, as much leisure as she. I had no idea what excuse I would give for not returning to work on time, but I put the question from my mind. I had the sensation that I had earned Jenny's presence by this dereliction; it was a truancy that framed and accentuated the pleasing unnaturalness of the situation.

So we passed beneath shadow-patches of sycamore leaves and out again, as if on a swing, into the spring sunlight, which seemed made to hold the lives of strangers in a harmony like familiarity, until we came to Millie's Diner, which we entered.

There we had coffee and pecan pie. There's a greenish haze to Millie's Diner. The interior is a little gloomy, and the glass front is shaded by leaves. The furnishings are mainly dark wood, which seems to emanate a calm, sober silence the way some clocks do. Together, the green and the gloom create a different world, like an aquarium. Only, instead of being filled with water, the environment of Millie's Diner is different to the world outside because it's filled with foreign memory. Mind, I don't say 'memories'—'memory,' uncountable and general, like water. Foreign, because the memory doesn't seem to belong to your own life, even in atmosphere.

Despite this sense of seclusion—subconsciously, perhaps one reason I'd thought of the place—those large sheets of window glass left us clearly visible to anybody passing on the sidewalk. There was no reason someone from the office should be walking by there at that time of day, but I could not help thinking of it.

Potentially, there is something like a science to dreaming—I mean figuratively dreaming—and to realising one's dreams. If so, I must be a pioneer in that science by now. This is one principle of dreaming I would propose, based on experience: on the occasions when life seems to have strayed—wonderfully—into dream, a reaction soon sets in to the initial delight, and the subject will deliberately behave as if living in the most mundane reality (somewhat in the manner of the cliché of a person whistling to himself to feign innocence). This is partly to test the truth of the dream, to see if mundane things will wake the subject up. Anything 'too good to be true' is eventually tested in this way. This testing, in itself, has a double purpose: on the one hand, the subject desires more than anything that the dream is real, and therefore seeks the security of knowledge; on the other, he (in this case 'he') wants disappointment sooner, while it is still bearable, if it must come. There is also a possible third purpose—what is wished for, long since defined as unreal, might seem, now that it has arrived, dizzying, frightening, positively weird, and reality—long despised—suddenly appears a reassuring home.

But there is another reason, apart from testing, that the dreamer will act in a mundane manner. It is a reason apparently conflicting with the above, though both reasons can co-exist in the same heart (such is our peculiar relationship with dream). The dreamer, in becoming excessively aware of the dream and of his delight in it, thereby seems to transform it into a fragile soap bubble. Just as a child, wishing to hold but not to destroy the precious iridescence of such a bubble, will shepherd it gently about in the cage of his fingers, hardly daring to move at all, so will the dreamer apply the brakes of mundane behaviour, hoping to eliminate any sudden movement that might burst the dream.

For all of these assorted reasons, and probably for others, what I first spoke about after we sat down together had a professional tone about it.

"I'm looking for work, too," I said. "I'm always looking for work."

"You don't have a job?"

I smiled. She could have taken the smile to mean, "If I had a job, would I be drinking coffee and eating pecan pie at this time of day?"

"I have a job. I'm a draughtsman. But my real work is not that simple. In a way, my real work is something that doesn't exist yet. That's what I mean—looking for work."

"You sound like a man with a dream, Mr. Winton."

I know she added "Mr. Winton" at the end because the sentence would have been too blunt without it, but it bothered me. At the same time, her mention of something that was on my mind—dreams—seemed evidence of an intelligent sympathy working within the details of the situation.

"Doesn't everyone have a dream?"

She shook her head.

"Some people don't."

"How do you know that?"

"How do you know they *do*?"

"I… I suppose I don't."

"You see."

"Wait a minute. You're not telling me you're 'some people,' are you?"

"Why not?"

"Because I don't believe it."

"Really?"

This was perplexing. I realised something at that moment. Wishing someone well—isn't that 'farewell'? And 'good luck'—isn't that 'goodbye'? There was something like this in saying I was a man with a dream. I half-believed what she implied, maybe more than half, but even if an itch is just on a tiny pinpoint of your skin, it can make your whole body shiver. And so, a tiny niggle screwed up all my other feelings around it. Somehow—I thought—she was lying. It wasn't just a plain lie. She was a pretty girl and a healthy girl, but she had been hurt or shamed or *something*, and so she thought that the healthiest thing of all was to pretend she never had a dream. But wait… I am using too many words—I believed she was afraid.

"You must have a dream."

"I don't see why."

I smiled again. If her riddle was deliberate, then she was getting the better of me. But I also had a fleeting instinct that this conversation had occurred before, that it would occur again. I seemed to be watching it occur in endless repetitions like the reflections in opposed mirrors. It was the most tenuous of sensations, and yet it contained a world of philosophy and sub-sensations, distinct as microscopic organisms in a drop of water. In other words, this conversation was a kind of eternity, and although eternity winked at me with the sympathy I'd felt when Jenny first mentioned dreams, yet I was maddened by helplessness.

"Because," I said, seeming to gain control of my smile and the conversation with it, "we've already established that you're Jenny Mills. Some people don't dream, but

Jenny Mills is not 'some people.' *Ergo,* Jenny Mills has a dream."

"If you put it like that, you must be right."

"That's a classical education."

"Is that so?"

"You did meet me at the Museum."

"Yes. In that case, you should tell me what my dream is, since I don't seem to know for myself."

"I'd like to… Have you ever thought of being an actress?"

"Nooo." She shook her head, drawing out the 'o' in her reply as if being patient with a question to which I had surely known the answer before I asked.

Now that I'd said it, in Jenny's presence, it did seem, somehow, an empty suggestion—puerile.

"A dancer?" That seemed more like it, but she shook her head again.

"Well, let me ask you a question. Is there something you like doing more than anything else?"

"I know why you ask that. I wanted to see a little of the world, and I wanted to do things for myself, so I came to Brookdale and here I am. I like walking the streets, looking in the shop windows, buying a new pair of gloves—"

"Going to museums."

"Sometimes… You know what—this is just fine for me. I guess someday I'll have children like everybody does, but I'm not even thinking about that right now—"

I wanted to ask her then if she thought her children

would have dreams, but I was in no danger of voicing this question. I tuned back into what she was saying:

"… Sure, I'm interested in things. I'm not a dunce, I hope. I guess you'll find this funny, but do you know what I think maybe I like most of all?"

"No, but I'll get my wish for today if you tell me."

She laughed as if being gentle with a bad joke.

"Trampolining."

"Trampolining?"

"I said you'd find it funny. The truth is I haven't done it for a long time, anyhow. It just sort of came to me just now. Most people get tired of trampolining. I think I could keep on till something made me stop."

At first I found this so hard to imagine that it was, in effect, meaningless to me. But almost immediately, I realised that the Jenny before me was simply diverging from the lines I'd drawn for her in my head, and with this realisation (creating, for a while, a double-image), the thing became imaginable. One or two times, I've been night fishing. To attract fish we break tubes that, when fractured, luminesce. That's how it was—something broke and gave off a glow. The same feeling as a previously blank-sounding piece of music beginning to be familiar.

In fact, now, as the melody of the idea hit that spot where it makes sense in the brain, not only was it imaginable, I could not prevent myself from picturing it.

"Would you call that a dream?"

I heard Jenny's voice, but I was seeing her now in mid-air, with red shorts and a yellow top, bouncing in such a way that the blood gave her pale, shaken legs an angrier whiteness still, mustarding her complexion with ruddiness.

A dream, I supposed, is something that gives you room. Without a dream, you have a single outline, and you can't escape it. With a dream, you have at least a second outline, larger than and containing the first. There's room for movement and meaning between the two outlines. With Jenny bouncing up and down on her trampoline inside my head, I saw ripples form around her, motion lines like those I would draw in a comic book. Were these not extra outlines of the kind I ascribed to dream?

"Maybe anything can be a dream, if you look at it right."

For the remainder of our conversation, I could not keep the idea out of my mind that the girl in front of me was deliberately maintaining a close fit inside a single outline, either with great and nervous effort, or with mocking ease. That jarring tingle I'd felt earlier had persisted and, by the end, become something else. It was distinctly sugary now, and had moved some way towards a throb. There was something hooky about it—barbed. I became aware of two things: first, that for a while I had been thinking of Jenny and not Lara; and second, that some kind of fishhook had snagged in the tides of my blood, and I would feel it rip the fabric that was the rhythm and flow of my inner life—body and soul—if too much time elapsed without me seeing Jenny again.

Soon I would hit the brick wall of our parting—I had to think and act quickly. It was no good, I knew, simply giving her my business card and hoping she would make the next move. Something definite was needed. Since it was Lara who had drawn me to Jenny, silently I now invoked Lara's aid. As I did so, something occurred to me that seemed so apposite, I almost backed away from it in caution. I hesitated, then approached it slowly.

"There's a theatre just a few blocks away from the park where they're showing one of the animated features I worked on."

"Which one?"

"*A Few Quick Facts About Mammals*. It's a supporting feature. The main feature is *Cat-Women of the Moon*. Would you—"

"Sure."

I nodded once, assimilating her affirmative.

"There's an early evening showing on Thursday," I ventured.

When I was alone again, I wondered if I should go to the office for the hour or so that remained. I decided a complete failure to appear would be more difficult to get away with in the end, though I did not relish facing Mr. Crabstone, my immediate superior. At first I felt like dragging my feet, but found myself walking briskly. Since I had no good excuse for my absence, I concluded that I must devise the most outlandish excuse I could while remaining within the bounds of plausibility. A scenario occurred to me and I began to imagine it with such feeling and thoroughness I hardly saw the streets around me. I entered into my own psychic theatre, living it, so that the lines I rehearsed for the office would not be a lie.

The thundercloud that oppressed me did not break. My dread was only heightened by the ease with which the office door opened. Mr. Crabstone enquired where I'd been and I explained there had been a man on a ledge on the fifth floor of a building.

"And that made you late coming back?" he asked.

"Yes," I said earnestly. "I must have spent a couple of hours trying to persuade him to jump."

He looked at me oddly.

"Well, I hope you'll have those designs ready for me by Friday."

I said I would, glad to incur no immediate penalty.

When I arrived home that evening, later than usual, I was in an abstracted mood. Or perhaps a mood of vacancies and overlappings. The early spring air was turning blue. In that colour it seemed the various disparate elements of my life, and the expectations they engendered, might be united, but only in some synthesis of higher and unexpected unreality. I wondered how necessary it was for me to keep my current job. That evening blue absorbed its importance. My job was a mere form, like other forms I played with on my drawing board. Even if the forms played with me, rather than vice versa, this would perhaps only appear the intolerable burden of work until I recognised it as play.

I felt a significant period of time had passed since the last occasion and the moment was now right, and I went over to my bookshelf again, to extract that volume that created such a curious sense of interval in my life: *Magic Daoism: Volume II.* I read:

> The soundboard of a guitar amplifies the sound of the strings. It is concentrating the work done by the air. Without the air, the strings could not vibrate and thus make music. In life, the physical, sensory fact of here-and-now is like the strings of a guitar. It could not make music—that is, be aware of itself—in any meaningful way without the elsewhere that is the soundboard. But what does elsewhere correspond to? Not one thing only. Some speak of nothingness or void performing this function. For others, it is imagination. Others still refer to further permutations of elsewhere. We are here concerned with void and with imagination. The void experience of elsewhere is often characterised by an expansive sense of indifference; the imaginative experience of elsewhere, on the other hand, has a peculiar, thrilling catch to it.
>
> Let us imagine a portal, one side of which is here-and-now and one side of which is elsewhere. When we become aware of elsewhere, we feel the influx of elsewhere-air, a liberating emptiness. But some find mixed with this air a flavour, an incense, the smoke

of a burning spice. The air itself—void—is easier to describe, though notoriously ineffable, since it is free of specific qualities and therefore may be fairly identified in terms of symptoms. The smoke, however, also ineffable, nonetheless has specific, consistent qualities. It is not enough to say what it is not, and yet what it *is* remains resistant to even the most ingenious, delirious, articulate and intuitive poets' attempts at description. Some guiding symbolic words, however, have been considered useful. Chief among these are: magic, *sehnsucht*, and, of course, blue.

How far, I began to wonder, could I truly play with the forms of things? Not just in my mind, but in real life? That issue of the *Brookdale Examiner* caught my eye, folded open at a particular page with a particular address circled in blue ink. I was sitting at my desk now and I pulled out a drawer to my left. It contained many sheets of letter-writing paper, envelopes, ink, a fountain pen, etc. Assembling these materials and constructing a letter is a very manual business. One implements one's ideas directly upon paper. Flexible in its simplicity, letter-writing requires intelligence. Through limits to the limitless. I set about my task.

However it had originally come about, it began to seem almost natural that I was seeing Jenny Mills—almost, but not. That is, I did not question the fact of it happening, but I did wonder how long such a fact could endure. Hailstones sometimes fall on a summer's day, and we don't call them a miracle; we do expect them to be gone soon. Nonetheless, there was something in me that wanted to get this hard-boned ghost permanently into my life, to make this strange, talking outline a fixture. Sometimes I believed I was passing beyond Jenny's ruby horizon into familiarity, even intimacy, and this sensation was another permutation of that first jarring tingle. Now red sugar seemed to have dusted all outlines like snow; it was dissolving with dream-heat and taking the outlines with it in a swirl.

Seeing Jenny—'seeing' is an apt word. My encounters with the person of this name, as well as the periods between those encounters, were an obsession of vision, and the details of vision, that vision and those details being closed gates on whose surface are engraved enigmatic glyphs the meaning of which—if understood— would provide the only key to open them.

Then again, sometimes she seemed like a projection from within me. A mental projection is the most inaccessible thing of all; it has a rainbow quality of elusiveness. It feels no need to return whence it came, but for you, the one who projects, to claim it is to lose it. It smiles and purrs with the advantage it has over you.

I don't intend to imply that Jenny really was a projection. Even now I don't think that exactly, but she was holographic with the same paradoxes as a projection would be. In fact, after two or three meetings, I began to think of her as 'the marshmallow diamond' since it was a cross between those two uncrossable things that she most brought to mind. I'll give an example or two to illustrate my meaning.

That first Thursday evening, after we went to the film theatre together, I caught a cab for us, telling the driver to stop first at Jenny's address to drop her off. Looking back, it might have been too soon, but intoxicated by circumstances and the proximity of Jenny's firm, white being, I put my hand on her left leg, just above the knee. Nothing happened—but a strange kind of nothing. In such strangeness I could either withdraw my hand, or move in to the warmth and perfume of her cheek and neck area, like a fish moving into a reef. I chose the latter course. For a moment my intoxication swelled and told me it was the right—that is, the successful—course. But at the final instant, it seemed, Jenny flinched away, scrunching her shoulder and cheek protectively together. This, I think, was where the image of the marshmallow diamond began. Her action was so full of opposites. It was sensitive (I didn't even touch her and she felt it), yet it was cold (I'm not sure any words could have formed a more eloquent rejection). It was hard (the movement was jerky, angular), and yet it was of the most rapturous soft-ness (I could see, though they were hidden, the doughy wrinkles formed in her white neck). It was distant (for obvious reasons), and yet close (there was a sense she acted only of necessity, without disdain, as well as which, she made no attempt to remove my hand, which I removed myself out of shame). There were other such opposites—cruelty and innocence, calculation and unconsciousness, and so on. A marshmallow diamond.

I don't know exactly what I thought on that occasion, as I've thought so much about it since then that the event seems overlaid with many different veils of meaning and emotion. If I try to live that moment afresh in my mind, it seems first there is the unexpected barrier, then there is my injured withdrawal, and then there is the slowly resurgent hope, like a shocked snail's eye unrolling. Hope had to return—quickly or slowly—and it did so by my considering the rejection one-off or temporary. In fact, whatever the emotional obstacle was, it was never removed or surmounted. Instead, a state of ambiguity was extended and developed.

Jenny consented to take my arm—she corrected me that a man does not take a lady's arm—and even held my hand sometimes in a fundamentally unorthodox manner. And yet she was as skittish as a schoolgirl about anything more. I do not believe this was coquetry. The palms of her hands could be so warm they were positively hot, and simply to feel their grasp was as if her fingernails dug into my flesh to send a pulsing charge through me of electric blood, merging and melting our hands so that there was nothing but the pulsing charge itself. And she would talk to me at these times of the homestead left behind, giving some little detail of how she would scatter grain for the growing chicks, and, as our blood seemed to mingle, surely—I think now if I did not then—she was not talking to a stranger. And yet that strange, invisible barrier was forever in place. I began to suspect—to the point of actual certainty—that something was natural to her that to me had always seemed a wooden social contrivance. For her—perhaps—there was in relation to a wedding, a strict before and after, and those things that belonged to the after could never come before if the bells were to ring glad and pure from one end of the marriage to—how unsayable—the other end.

I guessed at this truth like a blind man minutely fingering some solid obstacle before him. The sounds and odours about him are those of a summer-rich meadow and give no clue as to the nature of the strange-shaped hardness that seems always to impede him. The impediment coming to occupy the larger part of his conscious attention, he is startled by sudden reminders— the leap of a cricket, the thrum of a bumble bee—that he is in a meadow. So, for instance, when Jenny let slip that my initial portrait of her was framed on the wall of her apartment, I found it near impossible to fit this information into the terrain-map I was building in my mind of our relationship.

I've noticed that in novels and such, events have far more historical accuracy than history itself. This is the omniscient narrator, of course. I am not omniscient even regarding my own experiences. I did not keep a diary at the time, so I have lost all track of the exact dates. I'm not even sure, for instance, whether the following took place before or after I learned that Jenny had framed my portrait of her. Time's topography during that period seems the topography of fever. I have in my brain that it was a kind of 'anniversary,' though we could only have known each other for a few weeks. It was Jenny's idea to visit again together the Museum where we'd met. If not 'anniversary,' I am sure she had some kind of meaning in mind. Perhaps she never told me what.

What I do remember is enchantment accompanied by a sense of selective amnesia, so that I could not put the enchantment in context, give it a cause or purpose. Jenny, in the Museum, was an apparition, just as a deer is in a woodland glade, antlered with magic, and seeming about to flit away into the forever inaccessible. We came to the very statue of Zwila standing before which I had first seen Jenny. As she stood again where she had once stood, I was overcome. Was this, in fact, the first time? The other first time seemed eclipsed, or subsumed. What I recognised was a luminous and engulfing difference. Before, I had been disappointed with those pale eyes and lips as-if-crossed-out. She had been not-quite-Lara. Now, for a moment, I forgot the names Lara and Jenny, and when I remembered them, I still was not sure who stood in front of me. Then, of course, I knew it was Jenny, but it seemed to me that her face was different, fuller, that somehow I'd been mixing up Lara's and Jenny's faces all along, that whereas I had believed Jenny's face to be the deficient one, in fact it was Lara's that missed the true perfection of dream—a perfection apparent now in Jenny's features.

I tried to see if she still had those as-if-crossed-out lips, but at that moment she spoke and my gaze shifted, guiltily, back to her eyes.

"Sea Monkey Kingdom is right by here," she said. "Why don't we go?"

Perhaps at that time—unrehearsed and without warning—I was struck more virulently than at any other (yes, virulent, as if with a dose of worms) by the fiery-vanilla question, 'what is love?' Jenny's voice rang like a glass bell. Intelligent, fond, unnameable as the flavour of flavour or the meaning of meaning. And this voice came from one part of a wide world, and I would gladly have knelt down behind Jenny and known of her what she could never know of herself unless she had been the most miraculous contortionist, known—dear God—that unseeing vug of obscurity that only the mouth can truly know, though it may never speak of what it discovers.

I nodded, as if yielding to fate.

My hand was clasped in Jenny's and I felt myself taken. For a while, as we moved from one room to another, I could not have spoken without the reverence of the gut showing in my voice. When I did manage to speak again—my awareness of our interlaced fingers and their conspicuousness in the world a kind of pins-and-needles—my voice seemed to float without resistance, the conversational equivalent of walking feet that do not touch the ground.

"I know the Kingdom very well," I said. "I can recommend one or two things."

"Did you work there?"

"Not exactly. Just a visitor. If I told you the real rea-son it'd make me sound old. Kind of a… sea monkey's uncle."

She laughed and I took this as permission to explain no further.

"The only way to hear real sea monkey music is un-derwater."

"Underwater? You mean…?"

"If you don't mind getting your hair wet."

"I wasn't really thinking of my hair. I didn't bring my bathing suit."

"The show is called 'The Anemone Garden.' You won't need your bathing suit…"

I'd like to say a word or two here for those who really do take their bathing suits to Sea Monkey Kingdom, the better to hear real sea monkey music. Those humans who are not as interested in the music, and who would rather not be totally immersed, often criticise those who are and who do take the step of total immersion, as poseurs, and patronising poseurs at that. It's true that those in bathing suits are closer to the music, thus physically in front of and visible to those who are not immersed, but I'm not sure visibility itself qualifies as a pose. As to whether the bathers are patronising, this criticism rests on the idea that the bathers are closer to the sea monkeys while not actually being the sea monkeys. Therefore, presumably, the farther away you get, the less patronising you are, and—by this logic—the complete absence of sympathy is the most respectable thing of all, no matter how cruel or unjust, because at least it is not 'patronising.' No doubt intelligent readers—of whom there are few—will need no explanations as to why the whole subject of being patronising is poignant to me. In any case, sentimentally if not literally speaking—though twice I have literally been of that tribe—I feel I belong with these immersive bathers, understand them, and therefore wish to defend them. They cannot help their birth, or even the ideology on which they were raised; that they take interest in things outside their native ideology and try to understand those things, does not make them worse than those who have no interest and do not try to understand. Perfect they are not; worse than others, most definitely they are not.

I continue: It is a strange thing to feel connected to a person by warmly linked hands, but to feel your two heads are compartmentally separated—yet in their isolation immersed in the same world. Very soon, we had bought our tickets, followed the notices, and were being prepared for an experience that surprisingly few of the visitors to Sea Monkey Kingdom choose.

The Anemone Garden is one of a small number of immersive attractions at Sea Monkey Kingdom, which exist, mainly, in a deeper subterranean level than the more popular attractions. Those who are not prepared for full immersion can take advantage, instead, of the facilities for periphonic immersion. The central aquarium, where the performance takes place, is surrounded by amphitheatre seats, and, at the appropriate time, there descends to each of these, from the ceiling, the periphonic helmet. Each helmet is actually the termination of a transparent glass tentacle, the ultimate source of which is the cephalic aquarium itself. Sophisticated hydraulic technology is at work. First donning breathing apparatus linked to an oxygen tank in the seat, the periphonaut then brings the end of the tentacle over his or her head. The airlocked helmet is slowly pressurised and filled with water. While this is taking place, usually some general prelude to the main performance is astir within the aquarium, so that there is a sense of building anticipation rather than tedium. When all the audience have been properly helmeted, or, in the case of the fully immersed (within the aquarium itself), settled into their coral seats, a great bubbling, rippling dizziness of the quizzylimb (the sea monkey harp) starts up in an ascending vortex of sound, everyone spontaneously—but awkwardly—applauds, and the ornamental clams and giant barnacles on the floor of the aquarium, until now hardly noticed, suddenly spring open to release the sea monkey performers into their submarine arena.

Like clownfish, sea monkeys have often existed in a prehistorically ancient and to science enigmatic symbiosis with sea anemones. For this reason, the Anemone Garden is perhaps the most wondrous of all performances at Sea Monkey Kingdom. I almost forget the residue of degradation about the place when watching the Anemone Garden. More than anywhere else in Sea Monkey Kingdom, the sea monkeys are on their own territory, or marinitory. Their synchronised swimming has always and will always make superfluous the flailings of even a thousand dazzling-legged Esther Williamses, but when this twirling, opening-and-closing as-it-were umbrella dance, this sea-daisy-chain of sea monkeys, whose krill-flippers flap with the near invisibility of humming bird wings, is augmented by the slow-motion can-can sway of the sea anemones' chrysanthemum-myriad tentacles, the pulsations, gyrations, interweavings, dilations, unfurlings, metachronal-wavings, perpetual motions, revolving tableaux, ripples, eruptions, hide-and-seekery, crescendos, diminuendos and contractions, are such that transport follows eerie transport in the heart and mind of the watching periphonaut.

The periphonic helmet results in some visual distortion of this unearthly splendour, even though it is also periscopic in function, and the experience is certainly an adulterated one compared to full immersion. Some opt, too, to view the spectacle from outside the aquarium without the helmet, giving the visual aspect of the show priority over the aural aspect, since they hear the music piped through electronic speakers. Sea monkey music is designed, naturally, to travel through water. In this it resembles the haunting ululations of the whale's song and the angelic Morse code clicks and whistles of the dolphin. The rhythms of sea monkey music also take advantage of the bubbling swell and drag of underwater currents to achieve their full effects. The hydraulics of the Anemone Garden environment are engineered to replicate such currents. The music, therefore, has built into it, as a kind of counterpoint to its own rhythm, the ripple and wash of water (not just a rhythmic, but an aquastic—variant of 'acoustic'—effect). And this suits the slightly distorted view through the helmet admirably well, partly making up for the visual deficiency.

Many have compared the sea monkey style of music and dance to the Hawaiian hula, and it's not difficult to see why. The hula seems steeped in sand, surf and stars, full of the rich, wild innocence of the flowers strung into a lei. The squidoodle—by which name we erroneously refer to all sea monkey dance and music—also evokes a cosmos of sea and stars, of sand and flowers. But the view we have of the sea now is from within the sea. That is easy enough to grasp. However, by the same token, the view we have of the stars now is as if we were floating among them. Altogether, it is as if the stars have come down under the sea, there to dwell with such beings—not human, of course—as understand the mutual dance of sea and stars, who live, love, play, sing, in forests and bubble-echoing jungles of haunted seaweed, where anemones are the stingingest and squishiest of all gigantic and exotic flowers, and coral reefs are enormous, venerable, million-coloured castles, alive with the flashing spirits of fish, shrimp, cephalopods, and where vast chandelier swarms of jellyfish drift by like nomadic ghosts through nebulae of space-ocean otherness.

Perhaps the most haunting thing about the Anemone Garden, and about sea monkey dance and music generally, is the smile that seems to animate it all. Though it contains warmth, even humour, it is not a smile as we know it. Its biology and geometry are different from ours. The sea monkey word 'squidoodle' is used to mean 'smile,' but is not appropriate to the mild flickers on the faces of humans. It is the flexible and elastic grin of spring-heeled creatures who seem ready at any time to leap like sand hoppers. It is the underwater-hall-of-mirrors grin of a mind permanently boggled by notions beyond the range of human thought (no doubt picked up clearly by the sea monkeys' nodular antennae). To see those wide eyes—crustaceous, amphibious—and the pixie points of that gaping grin, is to imagine those eyes and that mouth the entryways of a flying saucer-castle haunted by sniggering laughter and ping-ponging forever through an interdimensional plane of manic colours in flashes, stripes, strobes and swirls.

Spectator to this squidoodle extravaganza, periphonaut, I was, in a sense, disembodied—the swaying of anemones, the aquatic lure of the quizzylimb and the sproingy disporting of sea monkeys, where my head should be. But even disembodied, I was aware of a hand, held by the hand of Jenny Mills. Two hands clasped were adrift together in the sea monkey cosmos. Headless, I believed our seaweedy minds were one. The blood and the skin of that hand, in their heat and pressure, transmitted to me the most perfectly transparent sincerity. In such melting, trust was too apparent for the word to occur in my mind.

Jenny did not complain, when the performance was over and the helmets had retracted into the ceiling, that her hair was wet. She squeezed her dripping ringlets with the towel provided, in silence. When she did speak again, it was to ask whether we could also go and see the more famous attractions. Of course, I agreed.

We returned to the upper levels of Sea Monkey Kingdom. Here there was less need to commit to seeing any particular performance all the way through, as the attractions were arranged more in the manner of zoo enclosures. We drifted from one to another. I had lost interest. That is, I was more intent on observing Jenny than on enjoying the exhibits. This desire did not seem entirely mutual. At least, the attractions of the upper levels were still claiming Jenny's attention in the way they were designed to. Jenny would look to me as if to share her delight in these new spectacles and I would return her gaze in the hope of claiming her delighted attention from them, and because of this mismatch in expectations, a tinge of puzzlement crept into her expression when she looked at me. Our silences, interspersed with these glances and with brief exchanges of words, took on something of the sadness of night between the last fireworks of a Fourth of July display.

We had just caught the end of the Kelp Club Shimmy, a dance piece that took place on a sweeping complex of rough-hewn stone stairways, and the grotto-stage had lapsed into the casual business of interval, the resting and preparing for the next performance. For some reason we lingered here, by the surrounding handrail, and I thought this was a good time to speak, to try and reclaim the mood that seemed slipping away.

"Did I ever tell you about Chattanooga Angels?" I asked her.

She smiled.

"No. I don't believe you ever did."

And for some reason I could not help hearing her words—though simultaneously pierced with a chill and hollow doubt—as their precise opposite, as if she were saying, "You know very well you've told me this a thousand times before, but, sure, I'll play along and let you tell me again as if it's the first time. I was kind of expecting it right about now, anyway."

Although it had nothing to do with our situation (this is not quite true, as it was the Anemone Garden that had put the Chattanooga Angels in my mind on this occasion), the topic I had introduced seemed just right for the moment.

"Faces change over time," I said. "I don't just mean each person's face as they grow older, I mean types of face come into and go out of fashion. We have some idea of this because recorded images are older than recorded sounds. But I think that voices change in just the same way. There's a kind of voice that's just starting to disappear. Have you noticed? Actually, it's hard to tell, because it doesn't show up as clearly in people's speaking voices. It really only comes through in a particular kind of singing, and that's the close harmony 'choir of angels' voice you hear in the movies all the time. Except you don't now, unless they're playing an older movie somewhere. The voices are almost pure, almost transparent, but not quite. You must know what I mean. They've got a kind of honey buzz and sweetness to them."

"I think I do know what you're talking about. The girl will wake up from a dream and look around her like she can hear the voices singing, and she wonders where she is, and it's the same old room as before, but everything is different, and she walks over to the window, and looks outside, and all the time these voices are singing, and then maybe she recognises one voice in the middle of them, and thinks, 'Could it be?', and looks outside and there's someone who she thought was dead, a woman dressed in black, with a bonnet, wheeling a bicycle and carrying a basket, and the song she's humming is some snatch of something from the Scottish Highlands, but it's also somehow part of the song she hears in her head. And suddenly the door of the room opens, and she turns around, surprised, and says, 'Clark!' 'What is it, Lara?' he asks. 'Why, Clark, but I thought you were…' 'Were what, Lara?' And then, suddenly, she turns back to the window and says, 'She's gone,' and you realise that the singing has stopped—all the singing, not just from the woman outside. And Clark swoops over and he says, 'Who's gone, Lara? Who?'—Is that what you mean?"

"That's something like it. There's something else to it, though. I guess I need to work on the definition."

Jenny's little soliloquy had unnerved me somehow. I was thinking that I had not—I was sure—inadvertently written the name 'Lara' on the portrait I had given to Jenny when we met. But I don't know if it was this that made me flush with a hollow cold.

I tried to get back on the track of what I'd meant to say, and had just remembered what I was leading up to—that if I heard choirs of Chattanooga Angels when I was dying I'd know I was on my way to the right Heaven—when Jenny's expression changed. She jolted in sudden alarm and then held her hand to her chest to catch her breath.

"Nearly dropped my tail!" she said, in an exhalation of relief.

One of the sea monkey stage hands, whose job was to keep the Kelp Club Shimmy enclosure tidy and make sure everything was in place, had crept along the edge of the enclosure towards us so stealthily that we had heard nothing at all and he had seemed almost to materialise out of nowhere.

At first I assumed he was only there by chance, that we were mere bystanders to whatever he was about. But it was hard not to notice his purposeful manner, and soon enough it came to me that the purpose in question related to us. In fact—to me. Jenny's alarm was, in a sense, a false alarm; it created expectation of a link between the sea monkey and her. But the sea monkey seemed to ignore her as he spoke.

"I was there," he said, as if I had been waiting on some intelligence of this kind. "I was inside. In the blue room with the spray music. Atomised flowers. I stepped out of nothing, like all of this, but no egg for me. Not this time. There was an old Kaboogle. Must have been. But the past is unwritten. I'm afraid. There will be halogen lamps, and my skin screaming. Somebody knew that something would go wrong. There are others like me—seen things and put back down somewhere else. What I remember most is the future. That helps me, keeps me strong. But I'm still afraid of what will happen in the past."

This peroration was long enough that it was becoming uncomfortable. Spoken in a sea monkey voice, the words had a delayed, double reality to them. First the aural shimmer of those non-human vocal cords—like a sea-cricket gargling stardust, like a shoal of fish U-turning all silvery, this way and that—was too impressive to let the meaning of the words stand clear. Then the meaning arrived, more powerful for the delay, and with the initial scintillation of impressiveness undimmed.

I turned to look at Jenny, to glean what she was thinking, but as if he feared he might be losing me, the sea monkey continued more urgently.

"You're there," he said. "In the future. And her. Is it her? Yes. There are dream surgeries that will explain it all. You don't believe me now. No. Of course. It's madness. But so am I, and I live. I was not born, but you can touch me. Touch me, see."

He extended his right paw.

I had no choice, I knew, but to touch it. Beneath my fingers, it was hard and damp. I realised that I had never thought of surreality in terms of a tactile experience before. What is substance? This was and was not substance. Perhaps it was surstance.

"What I say," went on the sea monkey, "is only as mad as that. It's the truth. The more you tread the truth, the stranger it gets."

I was aware while this took place that Jenny must have been witnessing a part of me that, for unfathomable and unframeable reasons, I had kept from her. And yet I was glad she had seen it, that this had been forced on her consciousness.

"The worst they can do," said the sea monkey, looking me in the eyes, "is set the past to trap you. Then you think it's all already. But there has to be not yet. Has to be, for us to escape and see wide open. I've got no past now. I need to remember the future so I know what's happened to me. I remember you, though. I just need to remember what you haven't told me yet."

And he continued to look at me. I could not look away. His eyes were naturally unblinking, but I thought there was something wistful, pleading, in their globular glow.

"I've told you," I said, trying my best to respond in kind, "but not yet."

He was waiting for something more.

"I don't remember," I said. "I'm sorry."

His head lowered then and he took away his paw.

"I don't know what will happen to me," he said, "in the past."

He was backing away now, retreating along the route he had perhaps approached us by.

"It was a good future, not yet."

He continued to mutter such things before turning his back entirely and shuffling off as if his interaction with me had been a delirium.

My hands were still tingling. They felt rubbery. It seemed the touch of that paw would never leave me.

"Do you know him?" asked Jenny when I turned to her.

"Not yet, apparently." And I tried, with only partial success, to smile. "And who knows the past?" I added, more quietly.

I had lowered my eyes, and when I raised them again,

I did not know who stood in front of me. The question she had just asked seemed to superimpose a question mark on her own identity. Maybe it was the bizarre lighting of Sea Monkey Kingdom, or the fact her curls were still draggled with damp, but for a while I struggled to add the features of this apparition up to the sum of who they were. Or maybe it was the other way round. I was trying to read a sum as if it were a single word instead of breaking it down into its significant parts.

As I recall, two things in particular absorbed my attention after this date (if I am remembering the sequence of things correctly). In my memory there is a period of mental or emotional retreat, or rather, of focus on things necessary to my independence and integral to my destiny as an individual. The first of these was the letter I had begun and abandoned, to put into motion a process of application. I took this up again. The second was Lara. I was nearly ready, I thought, to unleash her on reality, to see how the Lara-transplant took to the human imagination, to risk the adventure of letting her live. Sometimes the condition of being nearly ready is the hardest thing of all, and that's how it seemed in this case, too. One has to decide either to live with flaws or to hold out for perfection. The former means allowing causes for regret to become eternal realities; the latter is so close to impossible as to induce agonies of despair in the attempt. Despair, in fact, results from any failure to achieve perfection, either because you tried or because you didn't. To be almost ready is to be at the centre of all such despair—in the very throes of it.

That's how it was on this occasion, as I struggled with Lara and her first comic strip story, struggled with her origins as if I were dragging her awkward limbs out of the surf and giving her the kiss of life.

Largely inspired by the recent visit to Sea Monkey Kingdom, I had made some adjustments in my concept for Lara's character. I wanted to lay open to her the widest possible opportunity for adventure, glamour and picturesqueness, giving her personality without making her too specific in her appeal. Now she was a renegade Atlantean goddess of dancing (a decision inspired by certain representations of Terpsichore in the Museum, as well as Rita Hayworth in *Down to Earth*, a film in which, I have taken care to note, you can hear reasonable examples, momentarily, of Chattanooga Angels singing, at two minutes and fourteen seconds, twelve minutes and fourteen seconds, and one hour twenty-four minutes and fifty seconds in the 'Wait for the wagon' chorus). She—Lara—was a hedonist, but good-hearted. She was unruly, but had a conscience. She was smart and strong, but girlish. And so on. Bored of being told what to do in Atlantis (which still existed behind magical shields at the bottom of the ocean), she had run away to the world of human beings to enjoy the advantage her special powers gave her. I decided that she would not be crass—despite her sass—but would have the guile to use her powers sparingly, so that the reader would never be quite sure what else she might or might not have up her winsome sleeve.

Lara, I decided, being a dancer from Atlantis, was especially proficient in underwater dancing. Therefore she had swiftly become, in the human world, a star of motion pictures, those she appeared in being vehicles built around spectacular synchronised swimming set pieces. However, that was not all. A gymnast, an athlete, a mistress of disguise and enchantment and, moreover, of Socratic irony in the form of glamour-puss nonchalance, it was not long before she was attracting the attention of various behind-the-scenes powers, the first of which to approach her was CHEESECAKE, the Committee of Heterogeneous Experts Engaged in Special Explorations Concerning Abstruse and Kooky Encounters. Not of the human persuasion, she was suspicious of anything promoting merely national interests, but decided that she could use the offered role of spy to influence situations according to her caprice, and that she could remain as slippery to humans as a slinky seal. They might insist, bluster and threaten, but they had no ultimate authority over her, and somewhere inside, this spiritual truth was known to all who dealt with her.

The first serial was to be called *Lara Strikes It Lucky*, and was to be breezy in tone, focusing on plenty of wardrobe and hairstyle changes for Lara, and plenty of opportunities for different poses, including in these, as if accidentally, an almost liberal (but not too profligate) number of indiscretions of angle and of arrangement or disarrangement of clothing. In short, I wanted to create as many whimsical pin-up images as were consistent with anything resembling a plot. I hoped that the strip would appeal to both male and female readers. When I sketched out the basic story line, including the opening scene of filming at a swimming pool, some espionage in a submarine, Lara being assisted in her undersea mission by dolphins, and so on, I realised that there was no romantic interest. This, I decided, was not an oversight, even if I did wish to appeal to girls as well; it was natural and fitting. There could be no romantic interest for Lara Lovelily. Romance, in her life, must be sublimated into the perpetual and infinite radiance of pure, solitary glamour, as if she were the sun, around which all things revolved, ever without touching.

On May the 4th I received a letter. My editor at Jupiter Comics, J. Farnley, was so enthusiastic about the sketches and storyline I had sent him that I experienced a sensation like the moment when an aircraft's landing gear breaks contact with the runway of an airport. The plunger of a hypodermic syringe, filled with a serum of 'this is it!', had been pushed deep into the glass cylinder of the barrel. I smoked several cigarettes in a row after reading that letter, in order to calm myself for the completion of my work.

I was very glad to have such a pressing and a thrilling reason (thressing? prilling?) to take my attention and my physical presence away from Jenny for a while. I let her know I was busy, my conscience somewhat salved because it happened to be true. Secure, at least, in the interest Farnley had expressed in Lara, I set to work on what seemed now, given the time and the effort, gloriously inevitable.

In fact, I did see Jenny briefly once or twice before the intensest flurry of my work had passed, but was able to keep our talk away from the topic of what was currently occupying my days. This was instinctive. Becoming conscious of avoiding the subject, I had to wonder what my reasons were. The trifling circumstantial reasons that occurred to me did not seem commensurate with the underlying poignancy of feeling that was the motive force in my avoidance.

This consciousness was so uneasy, so redolent of unnameable guilt, that I knew I must do something to address its causes. There was a spectre here, I understood, that could overturn everything. And one thing suggested itself to me as the natural means of exorcising that spectre, though I did not know why—a visit to the periphery of Buena Vista Castle.

By now it was August—almost-late summer. When there is really only one unnamed battle being fought, much happens and little happens, and time makes way for the inevitable. Flowers had passed full blow towards blowsy in the courtyards of hotels and the ranked beds of public gardens. Soon it would be clear that the season was in decline, but the decline was preceded by a sense of timelessness like a river opening out into an ox-bow lake. Sometimes timelessness is a piercing feeling, like

recognising the string that passes through the many beads
of a particular kind of mood or moment. In this case it
was a broad, lazy feeling, and its strangeness was only that
sometimes induced by the sunlight in its omnipresence
and the trusty, unconscious, solid ground under walking
feet. There was the sensation that something like heat
haze would occur and would stretch the visible world
the better for it to contain all the invisible and formless
daydreams that seemed so inevitable, though not urgent.
Is this really life? (the daydream heat haze would ask).
That girl at the window of a house I'll never visit, behind
the hand-tinted roses of a picture-book garden? This
sloping hillside street lined with magnolia trees? That
stretching cat on the steps?

On a day like this we visited the periphery of Buena
Vista Castle. 'The periphery' is an unwieldy way of re-
ferring to it. One does not visit the castle, one visits the
periphery, and the periphery, boasting a view of the castle and only being a periphery by virtue of that view, is
therefore Buena Vista. It's hard to say just where Buena
Vista begins and ends (and this, too, is part of its design),
but there is a circuit, a perimeter, that gives it the definition it needs for its beginninglessness and endlessness to
be truly effective. This perimeter marks precisely how
near a person is allowed to approach the castle. It is a
line that the ordinary citizen is not permitted to cross.
The distance of this line from the castle is at no point
less than two miles. It is clear, therefore, that the castle is,
in height, comparable to a skyscraper, and surely covers
a greater area than any skyscraper ever built.

Almost from its conception, Mr. Skelton, the millionaire mastermind behind the castle, to whose vision the city had given their allegiance, had known that mesmerism would be pivotal in its construction. We do not know the full extent of this mesmeric influence in the building's genesis and formation. We do know that, among the few who bent over early blueprints of the castle on the desk in Skelton's office, aside from Thomas Perinth, the architect, was the illustrious Wayne Jaspers, the foremost conjuror, illusionist, escapologist and practitioner of mesmeric arts in the whole of the ASAF. Given a prominent place in the publicity for the building was the fact that its projected decade-long construction would have to be concealed from the eyes of the world until the completed castle and grounds were ready for unveiling. The veiling that preceded the *un* was effected—the boast went—by the unfathomable manipulations of Wayne Jaspers, who extended the web-weaving of illusion to the wondrous limits of that art in order that nothing of the process of construction would be glimpsed by the uninitiated. Not only this, the initiated, too, were brought under the mesmeric influence.

Wayne Jaspers personally trained a legion of hypnotists in order to facilitate the necessary psychic airlock between the construction site and the outer world. When those hired to work on the site clocked on, they would undergo a thirty-minute hypnotic quarantine, allowing them to remember all that was necessary to their work. When they clocked off, this process was reversed. All the specifics of the project became so unfocused in the mind of the worker as to be impossible to grasp and articulate. Jaspers, knowing that substitution is generally more effective than censorship, instructed the hypnotists to plant in the worker's mind a placeholder to occlude the actuality of the site. The strategy most often used—anecdotal evidence suggests—was to conjure up in the worker's mind a picture of his heart's deepest and most essential desire. The benefits of this strategy, it may be easily understood, are manifold. The worker comes to associate his work generally with his secret wishes, making him less inclined to talk about work and more inclined to get back to it. When he does talk, his story of what work is like will provide a suggestive mirage of rumour that differs from the rumours spread by his fellow workers, thus creating an alluring smokescreen—or butterfly-swarm screen—of multiplicity in which truth is either hidden in full view, or absent, made safe elsewhere by the distraction created.

Not all workers, however, were subject to this strategy. In some cases, the hypnotists seemed to have used stock images and scenarios. A number of workers could only recall their worksite in terms of an ornate box of cut crystal, containing blurry objects of pink, maroon and gold. For others, there was a scintillating waterfall, the sight of which induced a piercing feeling of being about, but unable, to remember something extravagantly meaningful. Yet others recalled things stranger, more grotesque, such as a chamber filled with human skulls and with song from hundreds or perhaps thousands of unseen birds. There was enough variety and mystery to breed, propagating itself through the conjecture that was occasioned. For instance, it could have been thought that those who retained macabre images from their workplace must be more accurate in their accounts, since those hypnotised had tended to be given extremely pleasing material to keep them from asking questions. However, temperament and the human soul—some were glad to point out—are weird and unsimple things. The bizarre scenes—for instance—reported by some, of the revels of therianthropic children, could easily represent the subject's deepest desire, the sense of ghastliness with which that subject sincerely regards it consciously, the shudders it produces in them and so on, being disguised ecstasy— the result of extreme repression. Even the drabbest of rumours about the castle interior and grounds could be, according to one explanation or another, and by accident or design, red herrings.

Actually, I am reporting now obscure matters as if they were equal in the public consciousness to matters more popularly known and understood. What most people are aware of in relation to those who worked on the construction of the castle—if anything—is that they came away from their workplace with varying tales of a mysterious and beautiful place, somewhat beyond the threshold of the world that we might call 'our ken.' The general public perception is of a benign fog of wonder, promise and hinted wish-come-true. Only the few see shapes in this fog that deserve to be called spectres. That is not to say that such perceptions are unimportant, but they are far from widespread. So the listener hears of

Buena Vista Castle whatever rumour is most suited to his or her ears, the common citizen hearing it is filled with the good and commonplace dreams that are necessary to a good life and whose function is only to validate without the need for examination, the cynic and the smart aleck hearing that the inside of the castle is even now a mess of building materials either unsuitable or surplus to the purpose for which they were gathered, the entire project being, in short, a mammoth of a white elephant, and that largely unnoticed, unrepresented member of humanity who sees shadows move of their own accord and reads in this the inevitable and eternal fall of the human soul into a pit of illimitable queasiness, cosmic degradation and absurd fear—to his or perhaps her ears come those other rumours.

And in this way, it may be seen, the Buena Vista Castle really is an admirably wrought, a superlative enchanted mirror, showing in its quicksilver with appropriate per-spective, proportion, light, all the nuances of the human heart, while seeming to show only humanity's camera-ready smile and best clothes.

As a writer and drawer of comic books, and an illustrator for animated pictures, I admire this. I believe I see the mirror close to complete, because I have striven for that mirror-art myself (and perhaps others have their reasons for believing they see the mirror whole, or nearly so). But there is one rumour above all others I have heard concerning Buena Vista Castle that, on reaching my ears, seemed to have about it the restrained, deep manner of truth disguised as lie. And that is the rumour of the blue room without doors or windows.

But there's nothing I can say about the blue room yet, if at all. I meant to write more on Buena Vista Castle generally, but mention of the blue room seems to have pulled me up short. Yes, Mr. Skelton had a whole array of tricks at his disposal, though to call them tricks might suggest they were commonplace. No. Only inasmuch as anything that exists and is known to at least one human being as a fact is thereby commonplace. Somehow Skelton had the vision, discernment and means to assemble the highest grade of materials and knowledge from such 'commonplaces' and marshal them so that the maze he constructed of the raw stuff of mere existence tripped and took flight, lost itself at an indeterminate point, leading fact into fancy.

Anyway, enough of background and rumours.

Wider than the circle of the periphery and containing it, is another circle called 'the Line.' This is a curious boundary made of guarded gates in narrow alleys and toll booths that are really checkpoints regulating all traffic that wishes to pass. It would be a strange system of barriers in any case, but it is especially strange to see habituated residents of this picturesque area—where all unauthorised aircraft are prohibited—passing through the gates with their groceries, or walking dogs, and showing their passes to the guards as they go. These residents, I imagine, are compensated in some way.

Jenny and I—that day the phrase seemed natural in my head—Jenny and I slowed as we came to the particular gate through which we were to approach Buena Vista.

Neither of us had even been as far as the Line before. There was a power of enigma to this barrier. It was this that made us slow more than the practical necessity that any physical barrier imposes. The Line was intended not to spoil the view; if possible, to enhance it. For this reason, we were befuddled by uncertainty in its presence. What was the procedure? Surely it was simple—identification, perhaps money? But not knowing the procedure, we must have felt that we also lacked permission. Still, the gate was such that the uncertainty did not have to seem oppressive. We could enjoy it—even felt invited to.

The gate here was set in a tall, latticed fence of wrought iron whose seemingly delicate patterns of curlicue and swirl were complemented by the flowering vine that dangled its leaves, tendrils and starry yellow blossoms from the fence's upper portions. We'd chosen a way behind the backs of houses, and the fence was taller than it was wide. With the sun beginning to decline behind its elegantly curving bars, the barrier was more romantic than prohibitive. It felt as if we were at a gate to something that might go by a name such as 'the Old Quarter,' 'the Forbidden City,' or 'the Inner Sanctum.' Prayer, a wish, the lighting of a candle, the washing of hands and face, the tossing of a coin or the ringing of a bell—all of these might have been appropriate ceremonies to mark one's passage here, as prelude to entry into a zone of different rules or expectations, different soil or sky, into a kind of roofless underground.

Our actual ceremony was this: we made donations in a box on the wall, we showed our identification to the guard stationed before the gate, and we clasped hands automatically, the way that two escapees might at the moment they know they've escaped, when our feet touched the ground on the gate's other side. And once again we were in a normal residential area, the way broadening a little into something that could be called an avenue as it descended the hill. Normal, quiet, but enchanted. Perhaps we were already seeing everything in the silvered pane of Skelton's Buena Vista, but each feature of this new, unordinary world seemed poised, and in its poise to have the detail of single snowflakes revealed as crystals in the soundless whoosh of a blizzardy flurry. A street lamp, lit, anticipating dusk. Slender-trunked trees with leaves as perfectly in place as the petals in the tangled orb of an allium. The clean, simple tessellation of paving stones. Serried window panes in an exactness of fantasy, giving transparent entry to other lives and spaces, while simultaneously shielding them with flashes and phantoms of reflection. Enchantment such as this.

But this was merely our immediate environment, and everything in it, despite the contentment of an almost painted stillness, led sweepingly to that distant (not too distant) but central thing that was the view—Buena Vista Castle and its grounds, the parkland endlessly shimmering with the breathings of wind, forever like the breathings of midsummer nights, and the sky behind the outlined building endlessly scintillating with the here-and-there magic dust of stars or fireworks, or some other strange and glittery aurora.

With this in sight, hardly conscious of the movement—or existence—of our feet (perhaps Jenny was conscious of hers, but I was conscious of neither hers nor mine), we came to Buena Vista itself, the perimeter of the castle grounds, beyond which boundary it was forbidden to pass. The perimeter was circled by a wide pavement, and it was as clear as if signposted that we were expected to promenade along this in an orderly manner while looking... 'wistfully' is the wrong word. We were not meant to be wistful. We were meant to be enraptured. In fact, the effect was not anticlimactic, as it might so easily have been. But I could not work out why this was so. Filled with an inlay of golden fire, the minaret-like bulbs surmounting some of the largest towers seemed light as the thin, taut, rubberised silk of a hot air balloon, as if they might easily have floated away into dreaming outer space had not the castle walls, stretching balleticly, fastened them to the earth like guy ropes. It seemed wrong even to call the castle a building. In sheer size it was a wonder, an imposition on the waking world, but added to this impression was the fact that it appeared as if fashioned by superhuman arts from a single piece of marbled luminescent mist.

It was difficult even to imagine that this gigantic object might contain rooms and passages. It had more the appearance of a gaseous planet, like Jupiter. Naturally, this was the intended effect. If a person first found the castle opaque, they would then be overtaken by the feeling that it might really contain anything, imaginable or not.

Then there were the grounds. These were parkland, but of a densely wooded type. Patches of open lawn existed only in intermittent pockets. Such was the spell of the place that this seemed natural (and, of course, it isn't unheard of). In memory, however, I am impressed with the exactness of the design, in spirit as much as in detail. The grounds developed the mysterious opacity of the castle itself into an intermediate zone of hint and suggestion. The absence of people from this park was eerie, or at least otherworldly. There were animals, however, dreamlike in their conspicuousness. Miniature lakes of intensely calm enamel blue were to be glimpsed at certain points between the clumped trees, and glowing pink flamingos crowded at their margins, on occasion breaking into feathery cirri of flight above the trees' low, dark canopy. Deer were also present, flitting into and out of view with the tender innocence in their motions of things purely wild. At other times one might spy a chipmunk, a tapir, a peacock, a lemur, or some other such jewel of the kingdoms of fowl and beast. The flitting and flapping of these creatures ushered the eye into the depths of the irregularly ranked trees, to seek what else might be loitering there. But signs of human life were at best indefinite.

There were lights among the trees, globes which sometimes formed straight, dotted lines, and sometimes one or two of these lights would move, breaking the line, and since they appeared to be artificial lights, human agency was conjured in the mind. However, any people present in the parkland must have been unusually skilled in the arts of concealment, since an actual human figure never became visible.

It was not only lights that teased in this way. There were, too, fountains and flowerbeds to be glimpsed in little clearings, the former perfect for lovers' trysts and the latter surely requiring the daily attention of a gardener. Such was the uncanny nature of the human absence from this artificial environment that imagination almost became vision. A trick was being played, of some kind, and as a result—by design, it seemed—the onlooker's eyes would join in with the playing of tricks, and a fluttering sleeve would turn out to be a pelican's extended wing, or even nothing at all.

We strolled the perimeter just outside this pristine otherness. Most expressive of the accomplishment the castle and grounds represented was the fact that it seemed possible to divide the inside and outside (the otherness and thisness) so clearly with a line—the actual line marked by fences, railings and so on. Where the physical barrier of division was low, to allow those perambulating better views, I felt I could raise my hand, reach out, and touch a force field. Of what? Longing, strangeness, the manifold redundancy and peace of perfection. Et cetera. But, of course, the main function even of the enchanted parkland to our right (as we circled it in what must have been a clockwise direction), was the creation of distance, the making sure that the castle was always a vista. (Close to the distance-making park, it occurred to me that among the greatest secrets of Buena Vista Castle was the secret of how the other secrets were kept.)

From the start, I had been self-conscious about holding hands with Jenny. This gesture, deed, whatever-it-was, struck me as an anachronism. It was magnetic in both an attractive and a repellent sense. I have mentioned already that the blizzardy, smudged borders of the ASAF's origins have retained a fascination for me though they seem forgotten by most other citizens of the ASAF. For some reason it was of those boundaries that I thought—and with a sense I was missing some puzzle-piece—when I held hands, or wanted to hold hands, with Jenny, or when I avoided holding her hand. The anachronism of holding hands, the static-snow electricity of it, was not anachronism as defined by either a belonging to the past or the future, as we commonly know those concepts, but by a belonging to certain correlatives of time implied in the fuzziness of the borders of the ASAF (where clocks do not work and where spookiness illuminates and transforms all things like moonlight)—correlatives seldom and dimly perceived or understood at a distance from those borders. This factor in our relationship had compensated for any deficiencies. Jenny might sometimes seem two-dimensional to me, and as attractive but inaccessible as another certain two-dimensional you-know-who, but her hand, that buzzing, flexing thing-in-the-world, that—certainly—was as three-dimensional as it was five-fingered. (But maybe there's the clue—five-dimensional?) Now, at Buena Vista, my consciousness of that hand, and the troubling turbulence it commanded between the poles of attraction and repulsion, was stronger than ever. I almost feared it, as an animal does an electric fence. But I think I feared more that it would disappear, out of reach, suddenly and forever.

Therefore, as we walked and paused along the Buena Vista promenade, and as a tint of dusk spread too stealthily for us to catch its operations, I felt myself fidgety and irked around that hand. Certain illnesses make it hard to swallow food, as if the act of eating has become unnatural; my irritability was akin to this. I took her hand and experienced—not quite physically—a gritty, rasping dryness that made me wish for the relief of letting go. Having let go, I felt the kind of broken emptiness that makes a child sulk and cry. Before long there resolved in my mind, like the effervescence of an Alka-Seltzer tablet bubbling away to clarity, a very complicated and precise idea as to why this was happening. And in its clarity it continued to seethe. I said nothing about it, since words, even if they had not been stunned (which they had) were useless.

Posted at intervals on the railings were unusual notices. In fact, it was one notice, repeated. We stopped to read it more than twice, though after the second it was clear all the signs were the same. They read:

> Miracles are made of trust. Leave this ground
> untrodden for all our dreams to grow.

Reading these notices relieved slightly the pressure I felt in relation to Jenny's hand.

Partly—not wholly—I think I was relinquishing Jenny's hand in that manner—like a boy enfeebled but restless with illness—because I wished to stand a little back from her and include her in what I was seeing—make her part of the view.

People who reflect, struggle all their lives to put things into words. If they do well, sometimes they will feel they have managed a succinct hint at what they actually think or experience. Jenny at Buena Vista was the epitome of the need to reflect and of the impossibility of ever reaching the edges of one's reflection to define what reflection itself is and examine the very terms of reflection. (All communication takes place between people who already know, which is why we find logicians so exasperating—they wink without knowing it.) She was also, in that place, the epitome of 'things as they are' overpowering the need for reflection. She was those two opposites, because—so obvious I had not thought of it till then—she was a girl for whom there was no elsewhere. So, now, examining the soft Rushmore of her face, I felt myself close to the zero co-ordinates of all that begs to be articulated, all that beggars articulation.

"…the branch blossoms outside the window."

I caught the end of something she was saying to me. She was approaching, with the ghostliness of a lace curtain stirred by a breeze, a place where the iron railings, surmounting a low brick wall, met with a brick pillar, something like a gatepost, except that there was no gate. It was one of many such pillars at regular intervals. Perhaps because it created a kind of frame, or gave Jenny something to lean her shoulder against, she seemed naturally drawn to it. Her face was away from me, toward the railings and the park, but she turned her head just a little to direct these last words to me. I had the strangest impression then. I would like to say it was the very opposite of déjà vu. I had the sense that everything was starting with those last words that I had heard. Perhaps there had been a world before, but there was a complete disjunction between that world and this. This world was underwritten by no past of its own; it was borrowing a past, borrowing memories, fumbling in its borrowing, but essentially born of nothing, to fill a vacuum with burning and burgeoning strangeness. Those very words might have conjured this new world, since they seemed the spirit and the skeleton of its innermost nature. It was a blossoming. On a branch. Outside a window. And Jenny was a solid, flaming apparition who was the very opposite of the one I've been waiting for. She was not simply a mundane stranger, but an organised identity completely new to time, yet with the gesture of an arm, the arch of smile or eyebrow, holding up the vaulted pavilion of sensory experience.

"The branch?"

My words felt furred with slurring.

"Yes. I don't know what branch I meant."

"I don't understand."

"Nor do I. But I remember it now—every word, quite clearly. I wouldn't remember it at all if my mama hadn't written it down at the time. Strange how you can say something like that, and it doesn't mean a thing to you when someone tells you what you've said. My mama wrote down a lot of the things I said in my sleep and when I used to sleepwalk. But that's the only one I remember right now."

"Say it again."

"The whole thing?"

"Yes."

"Well, let me see. I did say I remembered every word, didn't I? It started, 'The second'… Oh…"

"What is it?"

A light had bloomed on the other side of the railings, and Jenny's "Oh" seemed kindled from its soft radiance like a flame passed from one candle to another.

I took a step forward.

"I'll be…" she said, and her voice was another little flicker of flame. "So they really do keep dreams here."

There was a comforting softness to her words now, like the hiss of a phonograph needle in the groove of a record. But that hiss was the very colours and texture of the scene which we breathed, spoke, acted.

I moved forward again and took my place next to Jenny, to look through the railings and see what she saw.

Not far from us, just a few strides away if we'd been able to walk over to it, was an ornamental stone fountain of tiered basins. Lights were arranged around and inside it to create different effects, but there were more than just pretty colours here. There must also have been a projector of some kind in or near the fountain. The illumination I had seen bloom in the corner of my vision was the simple lighting that made the water glow as from within, but added to this was a zoopraxiscope moving image, the exact but ethereal shape, in three dimensions, of a galloping white horse. Its hooves were soundless, and the waters served to obscure in part its pale outline, but there was a seemingly palpable strength to the tendons made of light that stretched and rippled beneath its wax-bright skin.

When I had watched a while, I was not sure I could distinguish completely between the movement of the image and the movement of the water. There was something in the way the fountain had been engineered that meant the horse's shape and substance were not only of light, but also of water. With the conjunction of these two elements, it was alive.

Jenny began to speak again.

"I know this horse," she said. "We used to call him Flash. He used to graze the land up in the hills above our little farmhouse. I don't think anyone knew where he came from, or who he belonged to. My papa made friends with him first. They were real close. It was like they knew each other. Papa took me up into the hills one time and said he had something to show me. We stood waiting in the twilight by a clump of trees, and Papa seemed to be watching and listening for things I couldn't see or hear. Then he said, 'He's coming. Watch. He's coming.' I didn't know what he meant, but then I heard and felt the ground thudding, and it made me so excited, I can't tell you. And then there was a grey-white shape, like a ghost, on the curve of the hill, and I was beginning to get an idea of who might be coming.

"Papa whistled then, and jerked his head back, and the shape slowed till I could see it was a horse. It was like it was the first time I'd ever seen a horse, like I'd never even heard of a horse before. I could see in the way it slowed that it recognised Papa. Not just that, it'd come to meet him. Papa didn't have any rock sugar or anything else. Not that I was thinking of that then. Then he came up at a trot and stopped right in front of my papa.

"Papa stroked his nose and told me all about him, how he was a lone horse and had just appeared up on the hill, and how Papa didn't know if anybody owned him. He said the first time he saw the horse was just a day or two after the big electric storm we'd had a couple months back at the end of summer, and with the horse being so white and having no home, Papa said he thought he'd come down to the hill in a bolt of lightning. That's why he called him Flash.

"I don't know how long we knew Flash. I just re-member going up on the hill sometimes with Papa, and Papa would know the right places, and the right way to whistle or call, and Flash would appear, always like he'd just come out of nowhere. And I always had that same feeling, that same excitement, like I'd never even known what a horse was before. There's one time I remember now with us just running, just running right alongside Flash, in the night, and laughing and hollering.

"But one day something changed. Papa had been up to the hill on his own and said something wasn't right with Flash. He couldn't work it out, he said, just some-thing wrong. That joy, like they'd always known each other, was half gone, or more. Maybe he'd get better, Papa said, but he sounded like he wasn't sure.

"Papa didn't take me up for a long time then. Anyway, if he did, Flash wasn't around. Then, when I'd almost forgotten about Flash—not forgotten, but almost given up hope—we went up the hill again, not expecting anything, and Flash came galloping out of nowhere before Papa had even whistled. Now I could see for myself, Papa hadn't been lying. There really was something wrong with Flash. I was so scared I could hardly move. Papa was waving his hand and telling me get back get back, and I did, though nothing had ever been harder for me in my life.

"I couldn't think what was happening, what was supposed to happen—you know, there wasn't any 'supposed to' now. I guess I must have trusted Papa would come back down after me, but if I did, that little thread of trust was so fine I just couldn't see or feel it anymore.

"Well, he did come down, though his hand was hurt. He said it wasn't Flash's fault, that it was the fault of stupid people. I never really understood that, though deep down I thought I did.

"And three days later, there was the most horrifying thunderstorm I've ever known. I thought the lightning was going to smash the house to splinters. There are some things that happen when you're a kid that you think, the worst part of it is that it doesn't kill you. You can't say a thing about them. You can't even cry. Well, somehow, for me, that thunderstorm was one of them. I knew then I'd never see Flash again. And I never did. He'd gone clean off the face of the Earth, or else been killed, which was so much worse I couldn't think it to believe it.

"You know, I've just realised. It was after that thunderstorm I began to talk in my sleep…"

It was strange, I thought, the way she had spoken, as

if she had known each word she would speak in advance, to the end. This quality gave a varnished outline to her story, the way the voice of a singer on a record is outlined by the sound production against the background of the musical arrangement, or the way the lines spoken by actors, in the same movie screened every night for weeks at the theatre, show themselves as something honed to a perfect echo in eternity, spontaneity and inevitability swinging in the scales with the repetition until a balance is reached where both disappear.

There was silence again now—the silence of dust motes in a movie theatre when a projector is whirring to a halt after the end of the final reel. A celluloid silence. I noticed also that the lights which had made the fountain glow were now extinguished, and the image of the horse had gone. The sound of water brought a sense of freshness and wakefulness to the hush and the gloom.

I drew right up to the railings, with that useless detective feeling that comes on me now and then in life. Only this time it did not seem quite as useless as it normally would. But the bars naturally kept me at a distance from the object of my curiosity. To use a little of the vocabulary preferred at Buena Vista, the whole thing appeared to have been a miracle of judgement, even down to the proximity of the fountain to the railings: near enough both to surprise and to comfort, but not near enough to break the spell. In fact, I was beginning to wonder even about this. Must one always worry about breaking the spell?

I noticed that Jenny was looking at me rather than at the fountain. I gave a brief smile and took her hand again, like someone promoted to a position he does not know if he is qualified for. Anyway, there was that five-dimensional, five-digited electrical entity, Jenny's hand, and now I felt myself, in dock with those five dimensions, becoming a walking, shadowy and autonomous extension of them.

I've mentioned that the barrier around the parkland was variable. The next thing I remember, or can describe as anything other than the flickering shadow thrown by a five-dimensional candle, was that we came to a section where we were no longer separated from the park by railings. Instead, there were loops of white-painted chain between posts lower than waist height. This was a barrier that even a child could step over, or, failing that, duck under. It was not a barrier at all except psychologically, or to a wheeled vehicle. Seeing it, I found questions about the parkland became newly provocative—more than hypothetical. One question was this: had Skelton and his allies truly invested so much in the idea of trust that there was no security at this part of the boundary other than this chain? But such questions suddenly seemed, like the chain itself, something to be stepped over.

I did this—stepped over the literal barrier—still holding Jenny's hand, but the mental momentum I felt was not shared by her. She snatched her hand away, tugging me a little backwards as she did so.

I looked back at her. We stood now either side of the boundary chain. She shook her head.

"I'm not coming," she said, as if it were something decided in advance.

"But, don't you…?" I started a question but was surprised to find no way through to an end.

Nonetheless, to stand on the enchanted turf of Buena Vista Park was not a disappointment. I felt the buoyancy of freedom under my feet. It was bewildering that such boundless confidence should be frustrated. But there was its boundary—the dividing chain. Ghosts and other supernatural spirits are contained by strange thresholds and seals. In some directions their powers are limitless; in other ways they lack the material powers of the average human. The confidence I felt now was a ghost confidence—a genie confidence. If only Jenny had stepped over that chain… Why *didn't* she? On the one hand, it was inevitable she wouldn't. On the other, there was no reason for her not to. I could tell that this was just the way it goes. Then again, I had the feeling I was missing something, that as a matter of comprehensive personal failure, I had not identified some peculiar, specific problem that out of context would be meaningless, but in context, if only recognised, turned out to be everything.

There was an itch behind me—a stardust reflex angle.

After a long and complicated pause, I stepped back over the chain. I was not sure I had done the right thing.

Of that evening there is a great deal left to tell, but inversely proportionate to the volume of what remains to be expressed is my desire to express it.

Let me say a few essential things as briefly as I can. First of all—or possibly second—to hell, I thought, with the concertina-ed layers of my history of thought upon the question of what was—one way or another—natural and real in my relationship with Jenny Mills. Secondly— or perhaps first of all—I now saw Jenny in more acute focus against the Buena Vista backdrop. Somehow, she had come to inhabit her own outline completely. This was what had been lacking before, thus confusing me. Having arrived, it confused me again, but with greater gravitational pull, the concentration dragging me in. Thirdly, the scattering and the gathering combined. To hell with it and right now with it. And so I was compelled to force myself to do what I never could before, and kissed the entire existence of Jenny upon the concentrated ring of her lips. And in that adventure to make everything to-hell-with-it good, somehow, from nowhere, inevitably, everything was dashed for good to hell, though wobbling much in its trajectory.

Even during the kiss, somewhere near the zenith of its sensation, the bursting of its tactile firework, I knew that things had gone wrong. My eyes opened and Jenny was backing away sullenly in nonsensical opposite reaction to the wonder that for a while, in the joining of our lips, had been ours for the taking, without penalty or impediment. There were words that felt like gasps, and there were haltings, implorings, evasions, downcast eyes, denials, firm and heartbreaking resolutions, words of terrible honesty, words of breathtaking but irrevocable dishonesty, sudden, desperate, thwarted impulses, sighing retreats, despair disarmed of all expression. I remember Jenny saying quietly, almost—which was most wounding—to herself, "I think I should go home." And with the angular magic of the castle's silhouette behind us, the darkening sky flickering as with the exploding shells of some hushed dream-war, we walked wordlessly back to the Line, our hands not touching.

Jenny acted with more decision than someone playing for reconciliation. I wished it were otherwise. But she parted from me with no show of reluctance as soon as she was able to board an appropriate bus. She urged me not to get on with her. When I asked if we'd see each other again, she said, "I don't know." The words, at their beginning, almost inflected towards hope and kindness, but, abruptly ending, left me with a feeling of cruelty.

III: Montage

THAT was not the last time I saw Jenny.

I don't know who will be reading this, and under what circumstances, or if I shall ever find out who and under what circumstances, but I feel now, before I continue, that I would like to ask the reader a question.

Have you ever, unknown reader, had particular hopes about another person—shall we call them blue-tinged hopes?—but found those hopes disastrously failing to the extent that you became conscious—certain—that a particular meeting with said person would be the last? The last, for how long? Let us say, for eternity plus oblivion, with oblivion being barb-wired and palisaded by sexual jealousy. But I haven't finished my question yet: Have you ever been certain you have met 'a certain someone' for the last time, only to meet them again later in more equivocal circumstances, finding that the chasm of oblivion surrounding their words and gestures is not girded quite so much as before with the barbed wire and palisades of sexual jealousy; and have you, finding this, regretted that 'the last meeting' had lost some of its savage purity as a result, and tried to tell yourself that, in its own time, the tragedy of that last meeting retained, unmelted, its icy teeth? In short, I think I am asking, do you believe that the one who said goodbye forever was a truer lover than the one who sometimes now says "hello" and then, meaning it or not, "see you later"?

I wonder about these things.

Now I'll tell you about the last time I saw Jenny.

The strange thing is, it was on a bus, some weeks after I had seen her board one, and since which time I had heard nothing from her. I had got on at a stop a few blocks out of my usual way in the intention of riding to a place in the south-western suburbs—Hyacinth Heights, to be precise. What I was going there to do has no bearing on the story I'm telling, but I'll mention, anyway, that I was on my way to visit a friend of the family whom we called Uncle Larry.

Boarding the bus, I was not immediately aware of Jenny. I am sure she was aware of me while I was still oblivious. At first, she was simply one among the two-dozen-perhaps unknown members of Brookdale's public who were passengers there. Her gaze was turned away from me, out of the window. I noticed, as I searched for a comfortable seat, how ordinary this particular passenger looked, with her face towards the glass. How is it possible to notice ordinariness? Yet, I did. And I thought how romantic it was to be ordinary. And then, like the curve of the nape of that turned neck, a line of realisation traced itself in my mind. I had noticed that ordinariness because I knew it, because, even if I could never have it for myself, in some peculiar way I could not now un-know it.

I thought I saw a flicker in the faint reflection on the glass as if she had seen me, or perhaps just a twitch of her neck. She did not turn round, however, and I therefore had to choose between standing there wondering if she'd seen me or not, calling her name, or passing on. The strangest of the three, I suppose, would have been just to stand there. Actually, I took a fourth option. I did not pass on; somehow I had passed the point in my life where such weakness was irresistible. I did something not quite as brave and right as saying her name; I did something almost as strange as just standing there. I turned, just in the nick of instinct, to see the seats across from Jenny vacant, and I sat down in the aisle seat, where she could not help but see me if she only turned her head. As soon as I had done this, I regretted it, but I persisted. In my belly was an almost confident sense of a wonderful, embracing sanity—the sanity of realised destiny—that would step in and assert itself in this awkward, tricky situation. Why wouldn't it? Was that not the purpose of sanity and destiny? And yet this sense never became confident enough to allow me initiative.

Until it did. When I spoke Jenny's name it seemed easy, after all, but 'easy, after all,' in this case was not confidence—no. Nor was it destiny or sanity. It was fatalism.

She looked round.

"Oh, Victor," she said, as if she had not seen me, in fact, until then, and only half-remembered me. But she sighed, and that short sigh told me that she remembered a great deal more than half.

I was angry then. It was now obvious that the part of the world known as Jenny Mills had become—perhaps had always been—impregnable to me. There was no angle of approach, no pitch of tone, that would strike some precious, hard-to-find soft spot and precipitate welcome, expansiveness, and so on.

"I… I think this is my stop," she said.

I was convinced it wasn't.

Perhaps this was why I followed her down the aisle of the bus. Realising what I was doing, she stopped and turned.

"Are you going to get off here, too?" She asked it as if incredulous.

"Can't we talk?"

"I don't think we're going the same way."

"We could be—"

"Where are you going?"

I gaped, feeling cornered.

"The drive-in planetarium," I ventured.

She almost laughed, and I almost hoped.

"Without a car?" she said. "I have to get off here. Enjoy yourself at the planetarium. I've been there before. It's your kind of place."

Again, those last words sounded almost kind, until they were finished. And I thought then—a most peculiar thought—almost that it seemed she wished me to ask one more question, but I could not, even to save my fluttering soul, think what the question could be. I was thrown back onto the riddle of myself. My kind of place? Should I disprove this? And she had been there before… not to go again?

For a moment, I was seized by a wild jubilation: surely she meant somehow to test me. She was trying to tell me that if I could find a car and make my way to the drive-in planetarium, that's where she would be, waiting. But it would only happen if I didn't acknowledge the plan openly, if I acted in the giddy heroism of silent trust. But as I watched her walk away, the thought that Jenny and planetariums and the whole thing was crazy became so focused it paralysed me, and I was flushed with a de-scending chill. Even then, I could not shake the feeling I had deliberately chosen to believe the idea was crazy in order to save myself trouble. Was I grateful, ultimately, that she had forbidden me with her farewell (if only am-biguously), as she had also seemed to when we first met? It was easier to be resentful. And replaying the memory now, I seem to recall that, whether or not something in her tone checked me, her lips at that last moment looked more crossed out and her eyes paler than ever, so that a quiver of despair squeezed my heart for a moment, and this, too, robbed me of momentum.

She, ridiculously, as I witnessed, disembarked, and waited for another bus on the same route. I saw enough to know this. I did not have to keep watching, and I sat down. In my mind's eye, I then saw Jenny Mills boarding the bus for which she waited. I was destined now for a seat at a table where mention of Jenny would have been, if not impertinent, then meaningless. Since that time, I have never again boarded a bus on which Jenny was a passenger. I know this because I am no longer able to board one without searching for Jenny amidst the general anonymity. However, because the last two times I saw Jenny in a corporeal sense were when she was boarding a bus and when she had disembarked from one bus to board another, I cannot help thinking of her as eternally riding buses, perhaps disembarking here or there, but only to wait for another bus and embark again. Moreover, since I see her as forever riding buses (looking away and out the window), and since I never see this with my actual eyes, I sometimes find myself passenger of an acutely real dream or vision in which Jenny and I are eternally in parallel and separate buses.

It is at this point in my life that something very peculiar happened to me, which I might well have expected, but never did. It took me some time to understand it, and perhaps I never would have quite, if it were not for the fact that I am an animator and comic book artist. My personal life was catching up with my vocation. One moment I was walking down an autumnal avenue, the next I was staring from the window of my apartment into a night chequered by the lonely lights of other lives. One moment I was working at my drawing board, and sighing, and laying down my pencil, resigned, the next my life had evaporated, to be replaced by visions of Jenny, bouncing and bouncing, and slowing to eternal suspension, in the air above a trampoline.

It was a montage.

One reason it took time for me to understand this was that a montage feels different on the inside to how it looks on the outside. It takes longer and contains more detail. You may wonder how it is possible to identify a montage from within at all, since from the outside it is characterised by the fact it is a very selective summary of events. This is not an easy question to answer. Perhaps it is partly a sense of disjunction, the feeling, at times, that a scene in your life has just begun, though usually in one's life there are no distinct scenes. Also, the various scenes, which you feel suddenly beginning in this way, like a very eerie kind of waking up, are connected to each other not so much by time and event as by mental and emotional association. In effect, the days seem to become no more than the content of your mind, which constructs time on a dreaming/waking/revolving/sifting basis. From the outside, a montage is brief and economical; from inside it seems it will never end.

Some montages are punctuated by periods of what may be called 'real time,' the way a song might fade out to allow some dialogue in a film, and then fade back in again. A montage may reprise itself a number of times before it finally passes, and that was the case with me.

The montage probably began the day after my bus encounter with Jenny, when, after failing to finish my lunch in the park, I began to walk among the lawns and flowerbeds. I was disconsolate, noticing how the park seemed to take me back to the time before I knew Jenny, only to emphasise that I could neither return to those days, nor recover her who had brought them to an end. My feelings had something of the stirring, circling quality of the melody of a song. The willows, trailing their ribbon branches in the pond, were the harp. The wind that tossed about sheets of old newspaper was the string section. The feeling that seemed always about to blur into tears was the guitar. My own heart was the bass. And somehow every ripple of water, every curve of path and blade of grass in that park seemed conjured by this nameless song, part of the dreary aching landscape that existed between the lyrical lines of its simple yet grand narrative. A song narrative and a montage narrative are essentially the same in nature: they function by rhythm and truncation, each scene cutting or fading, before its conclusion, to another. This was my first clue.

Certainly, I noticed that the world was different, but I thought this the natural consequence of an abortive affair of the heart and didn't soon understand the significance of what I was seeing and feeling.

Variations of this same perception and experience continued while I was at work and when I returned home.

I began to notice something else. It was distinct enough to be identifiable as a recurring perception, but it is probably impossible to describe it except in a symbolic sense. It was something like this: the guitar arpeggios that formed a lachrymose feeling somewhere about my chest and throat, were also in my vision, where they would jangle-revolve around certain features of what I saw—such as a window or a passing automobile—as if to sentimentalise precisely those objects. And these arpeggios were a kind of subtle kaleidoscope whose gyration turned things blue.

The first break in this montage came when I received a letter, perhaps four or five days after the bus encounter. The writing on the envelope was in a half-smooth, half-perky, and a half-familiar hand. I had not received a letter from Jenny before, but had seen her jot down a line or two in her address book, and, indeed, in mine. Halves, of course, suggest duality. I was receiving something I had already lost, like an SOS arrived too late. Or like getting to know someone who was dead. The perk I saw in the letters spelling my name and address seemed either crestfallen—a hooded perk—or else barbed, keeping me at bay. In that I was located in my own apartment, alone, the opening of an envelope should have been something I could undertake in perfect complacency. Yet, even supposing the safest outcome—that the letter confirmed what I believed, and everything between Jenny and me was over—I could not help dreading that the message would involve some new information compounding my existing injury, or… at moments of insecurity we sometimes cannot resist fears that, at other times, we strain even to imagine.

I mentally surrendered to annihilation and then tore open the sealed lip.

The letter was as follows:

Dear Victor,

I guess I was scared to write you and you can take that how you like. Only, please don't write back. Maybe it's unfair, but if you write, I can't say that I'll read it. Even if I do read it, I won't write again. So this is going to be the last time. I'd better try and make it good.

I don't know about you, Victor, but I feel hurt and confused. I feel like a line has been crossed that shouldn't have been crossed. I felt that, anyway, but I didn't know why. When we met on the bus that time it felt like we shouldn't have met—not that it was your fault or my fault. It's true I was mad at you, but that's because you didn't seem to understand we shouldn't have been there together.

Then, after that, I was just confused for a time. I thought I should explain things, but I didn't want to talk to you, and somehow wasn't sure why. And then it hit me what a fool I was. I should at least try and understand you, I thought, and do you know what I did? I went right out and looked for some of your comic books. At first it felt like our first date. I don't mean our actual first date. I mean it was like I was dating you for the first time the way it should have been. Except that you weren't there. It just seemed a really fun and exciting thing to do, to be going on a

treasure hunt for your comic books in all the
soda fountains and at the news stands and
such. It was like an Easter egg hunt where
the eggs were all the dreams of Victor Winton. I felt like you were even with me somehow, and having fun, too. But I guess that
wasn't true.

I found a few comics you had stories in.
You've really been busy, haven't you? Gosh,
Victor, I know this is going to make you
sad, but it shouldn't do. I could see when we
first met that you're a man with dreams, but
you know what I didn't appreciate—you're
a man with real talent and dedication, too.
I hope you're not going to throw that away.
You can make a beautiful and interesting life
for yourself, Victor, and give something to
the world while you're doing it. Sure, I know
plenty of people will say they're just dumb
comic books, but you've got readers, and
they don't think that. And for what it's worth,
I don't, either. I've got eyes. I can see. And
I don't think I'm so simple myself. There's
something—I don't know what to call it—
something really tender about your pictures.
It's sure they come from a kind heart. And
they're smart and funny, too. You've got to
believe that, Victor—for yourself. You've
already got your dreams right here in your
work, and you don't need me.

Victor—I have to tell you. I'm not Lara Lovelily. I found that first number of the Lara Lovelily story. The one where they gave you the front cover. It was a fine-looking thing, and I guess you know exactly what it reminded me of—that pencil portrait you gave me on the first day we met. I'm not her, Victor. I'm just plain ol' Jenny Mills, and I don't think that's something you can ever understand or will ever want to understand, either. It just breaks my heart to write this, but I know it's the only right thing to do.

Good luck, Victor, with all your dreams. I mean that, and I know God must have given you them for a reason. Don't go throwing them away.

There's no easy way to say this, but life sure isn't easy—so, goodbye, Victor.

xx Jenny

From the outside, the interlude ends and we cut back into the montage here, but from the inside there took place all those things that the sudden cut back to montage serves to suggest. You must know, and I certainly know, that I cannot write them. I will write only two things:

When Jenny asseverated that she was not Lara, I remembered first the transparent sincerity of her hand holding mine as we watched a performance of the

Anemone Garden, and then her pale eyes and as-if-crossed-out lips on that final bus.

And the second thing I will write is this: I felt angry when Jenny referred to herself as "plain ol' Jenny Mills." My anger almost justified her saying it. That is, it begged the question why I wanted to retain the esteem and the intimacy of someone who was capable of provoking such feelings of contempt in me. The fact that my anger appeared to prove her right in anticipating our incompatibility only made me angrier. Plain ol' Jenny Mills! Who can refer to themselves in such a way? The dropped 'd' is obtrusively an affectation, and how can an affectation be plain? But in this fribble of self-contradiction there was vulnerability, and in vulnerability there was the truth of the statement. Maybe she really was "plain ol' Jenny Mills." And this seemed the most haunting thing of all.

And, indeed, the montage continued:

I dallied in an unfamiliar diner at night, idly stirring my coffee with a spoon and seeing a strip of sidewalk illuminated by the row of ceiling lights inside; I was walking down a street and came to a ladder, stopping at first to go round it, but then shrugging and walking beneath it; then I was on my own at the soda fountain, where some soda jerk joked, and, inattentive, splashed the drink over my shirt front and apologised while I wearily mopped at it with my handkerchief and waived his apology; then I found myself back at my drawing board again, drafting a female face and becoming closely concerned with the lips, as if I were involved in some delicate but urgent excavation, and then my energy and concentration broke in a tiny mistake that spoiled everything so that I crossed the lips out, again and again, and scribbled over my crossings out, and then ripped up the paper; and then I was roaming the streets sleeplessly, my gaze directed at the ground, and stopping beneath some streetlight, finishing a cigarette, and flicking it into the gutter to sizzle and go out in the cold, constant, unconsoling rain.

And so on.

There were layers of rain. As leaves are torn off a calendar one by one in a film to indicate time passing, so, more and more, it seemed to me, the scenes of this montage were like sheets of rain, each giving way to reveal the next. And as I passed through veil after dissolving veil of lachrymose rain, I also noticed that, inasmuch as it formed veils, the rain was blue; layer upon layer—blue on blue.

And then I began to think of sheets of paper again. I thought of carbon copies—of how the blue carbon paper makes blue traces on the white paper underneath. I thought of my own animation work, of lifting a cel away from the background image, and of how the picture in one cel yields to another. I saw curved lines forming, which, in their frozen expressiveness, were alive, waiting only for more and more frozen moments, in layers, to animate that life. Those curves—I clearly understood—came out of the blue.

I could not help wondering about things—about the way blue was thickening in significance in my life, and about the very peculiar phenomenon of the montage, which I was now sure was taking place. And so, one evening, I took the book of *Magic Daoism* (second volume) once more from my shelf. I opened that slim volume at random. The leaves of the book parted at perhaps the oddest passage in an altogether eccentric text. It was a passage in which the author—or one of the authors—claims to be extracting from "a diary of secrets," though he does not name the diarist or give any information that could identify him. The passage appears to treat of the unknown diarist's experience of listening to a long-playing record of popular music, though the artist and the record are, I believe, impossible to trace. The dates of the diary entry are non-ASAF dates, and the *Magic Daoism* author hints that the diary is from some other world. Perhaps he has invented it:

> 9th Jan, 2013
> Months have passed since my last entry. I do believe I had a significant experience on the night of that entry, but I don't know if I can now remember it clearly enough to give a good account of it. I will do my best to give a worthwhile summary.
>
> I am writing about what happened when I listened, in sequence, to the two songs 'Lovely Tree' and 'Palm Deathtop'. I think I must already have been a little in one of

those moods where "age and the only end of age" were like a spell on me, rendering everything ghastly.

"Last night I wandered in a wasteland/I was abandoned to the snow."

This is an evocation of losing everything, stripping naked metaphysically. There is a feeling of immense sadness and lostness, becoming freedom, becoming something that we cannot name, but our mouth opens in an O to name it—let us say it is magic.

"You came through forests thick with tangled undergrowth/With chicken soup, a Twix bar, and some winter clothes."

The tangled forest is that unmapped, unpretty, dark, chaotic and yet entirely enchanted place that is the inner self, and intimacy with the inner self. It is cold, lonely—and yet mysteriously warm. The 'you' of these lines brings comfort—the perfect gifts that come from perfect knowledge and intimacy. In short, this is the perfect meeting. The two meet in utter obscurity, but that obscurity has the enchantment of metaphysical nakedness, free of the considerations of the world beyond the forest.

Listening, I began to wonder how such a secular fellow as Momus wrote such a song, but more, why I was wasting my time wistfully listening to a conjuration of the intimacy of pure magic. *Was* I wasting my time? I examined myself on this question. A Buddhist or a businessman—the spiritual and secular realists—would no doubt say that a dream is meaningless and worthless. And I searched my past and I could find no sign that I had ever achieved or come close to that 'perfect meeting' in the enchanted forest, no sign I was progressing towards it. Yes—I would grow old and die. That's all. Why then—weirdly, queasily, yet at least a little wonderfully—did that dream continue to seem to me the most precious thing in all life? No, I thought to myself, it will not happen. I cannot wait for it to happen. Not in this world of one thing after another, of passing from youth to age and death. The two people in 'Lovely Tree'—it somehow, nonsensically, came to me—were meeting *again*. Not just the second time in a chrono-logical sense—there is a sense I cannot de-fine here, but it is only when we 'meet again' that we truly meet.

This revelation—whatever it was—already excited me enough. I believe I already had the following vision behind my closed eyes: A stained glass window in colours of main-ly dark green, grey, silver and blue, with a suggestion of snowy landscape outside; and a figure—a knight—kneeling before a lady (perhaps on a throne) in what seemed a depiction of shared sainthood, radiating simplicity and gentleness with a steely glow. There may also have been holly leaves and red berries in the design.

The song ended and the next began. "The house of the dead becomes more and more real to me."

Somehow the song was about the same thing—the same magical winter. And then—I realised—Momus was singing about *meeting again*.

"Sooner or later, we'll all be there, I guess/All already no longer exist/Together with our friends again."

Somehow he understood. He and I were feeling the same thing. Yes, we die—and this puzzles Momus, who has to declare he does not believe in "a permanent soul"—but somehow the meeting again exists somewhere. Where? Momus gives a clue by hitting upon a time paradox: "All already no longer exist/Together with our friends again."

We're not there yet, and yet we're already there, with the friends who have died before us. Both living and dead exist at the same time. There must be a bridge of 'already/not yet', since consciousness continues, renews, while individual consciousness passes.

Perhaps I have not explained this correctly, and have somewhere betrayed a truth of undimmed magic, but I have tried.

IV: Striking It Lucky

LARA STRIKES IT LUCKY proved popular enough for J. Farnley to write a letter asking me for another Lara serial. At the time of the release of the comic containing the first instalment of *Lara Strikes It Lucky*, the excitement it caused, which was observable but not overwhelming, failed to make its way to the forefront of my attention. I had at last completed and sent that application, perhaps as an ultimatum to fate.

On the day the letter came from Farnley, too, I was in an abstracted state of mind, having just returned from an interview and physical examination at the Basil Wolverton Institute, where much of the administration for Dr. Ingram's teleportation project was being carried out. I had felt, in the office there, like someone undergoing recruitment for the military, unsure to what frontier of human experience I would be officially dispatched. At the end of it all, however, I was merely told that my examination was satisfactory and that I would be informed if my services as a volunteer were required. When, on returning to my apartment, I read the letter, I felt a little like a ghost being asked to engage in daily human chores. There was nothing else to do, however. Presumably this was the success I should be enjoying, or something like it. Anyway, whether in weariness or hope, I decided it was a good time to hand in my notice to Mr. Crabstone.

It had not been long since I had written and drawn *Lara Strikes It Lucky*, but I refamiliarised myself with the serial to see if I could glean hints thereby for a lively sequel. As I did so, I kept thinking of Jenny's letter to me. "I'm not Lara," she had said, but who *was* Lara? Considering I had lost Jenny on Lara's account—that's what I thought, forgetting that I had more definitely met Jenny on Lara's account—I was not sure the exchange was a good one.

Who was Lara?

I would need to answer this question before I embarked on the creation of the second Lara Lovelily serial.

I tried the obvious answers: she was an Atlantean; she was a dancer; she was eroticism abstracted from the biological need to reproduce; she was a winking redhead looking for a good time.

None of these answers satisfied me. She is not Jenny, I told myself, therefore she must be some part of me. But what part? I could not find her. She was there, all right—I simply could not lay my hands on her. She was a mirage whose cause and whose meaning I did not understand.

Something—I thought wildly—needed to be earthed. There was lightning in the vivid, sweet cloud that was

Lara, and I needed a lightning rod, to earth it. I needed to get the joke, to solve the riddle. I needed to know the kiss that would wake the sleeping beauty. I needed to bring her out of suspended animation, and into animation. I needed truth. I needed life.

Lara's lips were fully realised, true, and not crossed out, but something was out of balance here. My eyes were drawn repeatedly to that which, knowing the images would be public, I had treated, in drawing, with a kind of chaste respect. On reflection, I recognised that, inwardly—spiritually—I had averted my eyes when I had needed to draw those converging V-like lines. And now I recalled the advice of a fellow artist: If you are drawing a female figure in a dress, first draw the legs beneath the dress, then draw the dress over the legs. Only in that way will the dress contain something real. Lara was not always wearing a dress, or a skirt. Certainly, when she was, I had first paid attention to the legs. Sometimes—often—she was wearing only a bikini. On one or two occasions she was in lingerie. I needed to get beneath this layer, too— zoom further in.

So began my first nude studies of Lara. I spent some weeks on this. The results were commonplace. More and more I concentrated simply on the vagina, trying to get the subtle personality of the vagina just right, so that anyone would be able to recognise that this was Lara Lovelily's vagina. It was tantalising. Still something eluded me.

Blue, I thought. Blue blue blue. Curves. Layers. Animation. Atlantean redhead. Underwater dancer. Blue.

Heliotropic eroticism. Jenny. Blue. Vagina. Yes. Winking. Magic. Aquamarine. Blue. Drench. Superimposed. Teleportation. Yes. Blue. Meet again. Yes.

That was it.

Somehow—in a way that I cannot now explain—all the pieces that life had assembled round me fused together in the single realisation: I had to redesign the vagina. I had to put a blank sheet of paper on my drawing board and reinvent the whole concept of vagina.

This is where my work truly began, though the world will probably never understand this. What is left to them are some scattered comic-book serials which show originality and promise, but which are somewhere a little undeveloped, and, besides this, some artisan work in animation, for which I am not credited, and besides this many folders of sketches and assorted drawings. These last are of little interest to the public, I would hazard, being largely groundwork for my comic illustration and animation. However, their sense of diffuseness and miscellany changes to one of extreme concentration in the last few folders. There is even a precursor of this final sequence—the folder with the initial nude and vaginal studies of Lara Lovelily. All the folders after this one are different in nature to everything that came before. And yet, these too, are a kind of groundwork, for something that perhaps no human being but myself comprehends.

As much as was possible, I confined myself now to my apartment. The room which I used for a studio came to resemble almost a laboratory as I worked. On several lines strung across the width of the room at head-height,

I began to pin various images and clippings intended to inspire and inform me in my new quest. Photographs of magnified snow-crystals and blood cells, of the undersides of cowries and other sea shells, of the dewlaps of dugongs and mouthparts of manatees, the arms of starfish and the noses of bats, cobwebs in moonlight—yes—and the diagrammatic illustrations of Ernst Haeckel—yes— and patterns I had made with a kaleidoscope and some photographic equipment—all these things I examined, absorbed deeply and drew upon. Other things there were—pages of stream-of-consciousness produced after tasting different honeys, or coltsfoot, or ginger root. With the aid of a head-shrink friend, I also collected accounts of how men in their boyhood imagined the secret female place before they had ever known it. I used mirrors and made strange symmetries with the faces of actresses. I read botanical treatises and pored over the colour plates. I performed strange ouija with closed eyes, using only mind, hands, and other things with which I was born. I became intimate with a whole phantasmal galaxy of female undergarments. And even then, for a while, it seemed I was only dipping my toes into the shallowest fringe of the immense ocean of the great, unknown, future vagina, which was also the great unknown vagina of that ancient innocence before the onset of specific anatomical knowledge.

Some of my initial mistakes, of which there were many, arose because I tried to solve the problem logically. Form follows function, I thought. If only I understood the function of the vagina, I would be able to create the perfect form. But repeatedly, and at increasing volume, my intuition told me that this was only a way to duplicate old mistakes and stay caught in the trap of believing that that which is common or central is necessarily best. I had got things exactly the wrong way round. In this case function must follow form. That is, I would find the function by following the form. With the vagina, I had to consider myself a blind man. I had to feel my way. I could not imagine or comprehend the function except by minute yet courageous faithfulness to the form that intuition and the work of my hands gradually revealed to me.

And only when once on the blindstaking pain-curve of following form did I begin to feel I was, inchingly, then slipperily, making progress.

In the drawing I have titled, *The Macro/Micro Platonic Vagina of Infraborean Atlantis*, I first had the sense of grasping the general form of *the ultravulva*. There was heft and substance here, like that of a young planet forming out of fantastic gases. But I needed focus and fertility. I needed cosmic rococo. To this end, I sectioned the drawing into a grid, and made of each rectangle a new drawing of the same size and detail as the first (*The Macro/Micro Platonic Vagina of Infraborean Atlantis*). That is, I zoomed in. The first sheet of paper was 34½ × 24 inches. The grid I made was of six rows and six columns, so that the rectangular interstices were each a postcard size of 5¾ × 4 inches. These postcard rectangles were therefore zoomed up from 5¾ × 4 inches to the new sheets of 34½ × 24 inches—thirty-six of them. Then I zoomed

in again, though not with all thirty-six of these derivative drawings—only with six of them. Then I zoomed in
again in the same manner three more times and was on
the brink of a further zoom when my life became giddy
and foggy.

With blinking eyes I asked myself, is this the final
weave and substance of the ultravulva? I examined the
six 34½ × 24-inch pictures that represented my fourth
zoom in. I will leave these drawings intact where they
can readily be found—this will be easier than attempting
a description. I have one of these high-magnification
pictures on the desk in front of me, however, and will
offer a few words for the benefit of those who don't have
the opportunity to examine the pictures for themselves.
Firstly, something of my technical method. Essentially, I
was breaking down the kind of lines I used for the best
of Lara—those with real Lara quality—and fracturing
and then fractalizing them. The high-magnification
ultravulva evinces, therefore, distinct characteristics of a
Lara-flavoured snow crystal, with the fractalized curves
breaking out frequently into ornate mutation. The overall
effect is not unlike that which might have been achieved
had a jeweller used biological forms as inspiration for the
conversion of a system of subterranean caverns into a
cathedral consecrated to unknown gods. There is no time
for modesty now, and it would serve no purpose. The
caverns of the ultravulva possess a complex symmetry
that can rightly be called lapidary (or labiadary). Vug
pockets drip illumination from clusters of nuggeted crystal eyes or eggs and ciliated filigree whale-songs with

the corseted quiver and tight bowstring pluck evoked by the timeless quaint obscenity of the Scottish quim. It is as if the tenderest of infra-flesh multi-dimensionally knickers itself into a whimpering heraldry of seaweedy cleft gussets. And blazoned into this raspberry whirl, Rorschach kisses wriggle like bursting pupae.

The first time I stepped back to survey my finished handiwork at this magnification, I felt myself teetering. Had I gone far enough? Would I learn more by going further, or would I simply drop off into an abyss, a microcosmonaut who, hearing the siren song of ultravulva, had failed to lash himself to the mast of his purpose and was lost in a labyrinth of detail, tailspinning to the subatomics of nubile chemistry?

I decided to pause and consider. Perhaps I was ready to begin the process of zooming out again to a newly focused macrocosm of ultravulva, to build up from what I hoped were first principles. I would lay down my drawing tools and let my steaming brain cool, and I would consider the question again in the morning of the following day.

However, that night I experienced something which, because it happened mostly while my body slept, I must call a dream, and which I took to be the beginning of the fulfilment of my work.

I didn't remember going to bed, but I woke up there, as if it had been freshly prepared for me in the guest room of a strange house. Wondering a little at the gap in my memory and at the gentle strangeness of the atmosphere to which I'd awoken, I slid out from under the covers and walked in my bare feet to the window. I saw then, with a frisson of delight, an unfamiliar world. It was snowing, and the outlines of the world I knew, under the name of Brookdale, had been altered.

The snow was silent and thick—palpably silent—and it fell like a blessing which, though certain, is so infinitely delicate in the crystalline proof of itself it traces, that no one, even if they know its truth in their hearts, can believe it when it is spoken.

I had been a long time working on the sequel to *Lara Strikes It Lucky*, I thought, and winter had arrived without my knowing. All the threads of care that had tied me to the world now seemed as fragile as in a web of frost. I could feel them melting in little shivers, leaving me only this snowy peace, detached from all other times and all other places.

At length, I returned to my bed, feeling myself as if buried by the swift, silent accumulation of snow.

Some time—who knows how long?—after I had passed through the layer of hypnagogic sleep into the nowhere of oblivion, I felt myself falling. I was plummeting through endless darkness—down, I suppose, though it was hard to say—and through multiple membranes or veils. I flailed my limbs in great distress, as if this might help me, but, as I fell, the veils through which I passed began to give me a sense that I was not exactly alone.

And then perhaps I was accelerating, or else the distance between veils was decreasing. As I flailed, I wrapped myself in sticky, scintillating webs; trying to extricate myself, I became further entangled, until I was entirely wrapped, as if an embalmed pharaoh. And then the web began to eat into me, sweetly; it was cotton candy, and it was turning me, also, into cotton candy, before dissolving like magic, vanishing me. And the sweetness that melted me was also the growing sense that I was not exactly alone—stinging like a battery on the tongue.

And then, my struggling with the cotton candy web and with my own nothingness was translated into dancing—madcap arms-in-the-air, straight-backed, bat-winged, orang-utan dancing. And my feet were helter-skelter on a floor that had until then been absent, and which brought wordlessly to my mind the unobtrusive yet, in human experience, near ubiquitous enigma of floors generally. There was no sky. I was inside, whatever that meant. And the floor, and the surrounding limits of the environment were red, and there were other figures dancing all around me. A thin, bearded old man looked my way, still dancing, and threw his head back almost coquettishly, in an expression of abandoned hilarity, which he seemed to assume we shared. It came into my mind that I was a baby, though I did not know how a baby could have such an adult body in such adult clothes.

Turning my head a little, I saw another figure. She alone, on all the dance floor, was standing still. And she was looking at me. Her expression was soft, patient, yet focused.

The enigma of the entire room was distilled and made personal in her face. My not knowing her was the same as my knowing her.

I felt my involuntary dancing begin to cool and slow as my mind became engaged in the meaning of her presence. After a while, I was looking down at my straight, still legs and brushing the sleeves of my jacket. Then I looked up at her again.

"Who are you?" I asked.

"I am the owner of the vagina you designed," she said.

I nodded. I thought… yes—I understood. This was how Lara's face should be. This was… Lara.

"But I didn't finish it," I said.

"It's finished." She stared at me in wonderful simplicity, and then gave a little smile.

I began to cry, and was embarrassed, as if I'd found myself publicly masturbating, having somehow, negligently, allowed a private state of mind to emerge in shared company. I thought I saw the thin old man throw his head back again and cast me another look of glee, as if happiness had weakened all his muscles into an almost indecent friendliness.

"Where are we?" I asked, with a catching voice.

"We are in my vagina now," she said.

And with a sudden rush of tears, the strength went out of me, and I fell on my hands and knees before her.

There was more—I believe, quite a lot more—but the rest was fragmentary in my memory when I awoke. I wrote down as much of it as I could, of course. My transcription can be found in the same folder as the series of ultravulva magnifications. Of particular interest was Lara's talk—it was Lara—of a number of rooms or chambers "without doors or windows," and a promise made to me to reveal everything in further detail over the course of the following nights. I would, anyway, have made notes on the dream, but this promise on the part of Lara ensured that I was punctilious about it.

Whether it came directly from some forgotten part of the dream, or was transmitted by the dream in some indirect way, I do not know, but that night's sleep left me, besides memories and a promise, another gift as distinct as it was immaterial. The morning after the dream, when the mists of sleep had cleared a little, I found in my mind something that had not been there before, something as perfectly formed as a freshly laid egg. It was an immaculate idea—without entrances or exits. I felt sure it was nothing that Lara had actually told me in the dream, but there it was—the function of the ultravulva. The function of the ultravulva is never that, through it, you shall be born, but always that you shall be *born again*.

Wishing to examine the world through the eyes of this suddenly acquired knowledge, I drew the curtains. The snow of the previous night had not been a dream, unless this new day was; it continued to fall outside, making me secure in my withdrawal.

My excitement and distraction after the multiple enchantments of sleep and waking were such that I could not think about the specifics of further drafting at the drawing board. But I began to picture the ultravulva at the macro level, and to jot down strange meditations and enigmas in anticipation of the coming night, as if writing love poetry while waiting for a tryst. These, too, are in the folder of ultravulva magnifications. I reproduce some of them here:

Tinkerbell's panties smell of vanilla.

The two words 'Dale Arden' are the perfection of sweet, wild innocence: white as teeth; red as lips.

The hula hoop of Betty Boop.

I was afraid I would not be able to sleep. What a broken chasm insomnia would be, not letting me fall, when I should, into the directionlessness that ended with the unbridgeable and with the yielding leap of self-undoing to the neverside of beyond-the-end-of-time undone. I was afraid my fear would keep me awake and I would hit the flat dead-end of reality with its forever question-mark graffitied on its brick surface anonymously. But the restless flickering of my scribbles reminded me of Lara's promise; they were my way of treasuring that promise in my heart.

But how would I sleep?

Perhaps I exhausted myself so much in worry that I did not have the energy to try to sleep, and so succeeded. In retrospect, I have to say that I believe otherwise: that the promise fell on me when I lay in my bed, as if the still falling snow erased me from one place and recondensed me with a soft, pointillist flurry in some unconnected other.

Here's something I scribbled down from my second dream:

This time I was talking to Lara in some blue-white balcony, hung about with curtains that appeared as if made of macroscopic snowflakes. I do not remember the view, except as golden-blue illuminating far-flung crystalline magnificence. Lara was saying, "This isn't a dream. It's the future, and you're a baby here, baby. You'll be back. You'll see."

"The future?" I said. "I'm already here? I can't be, or you'd say it was the present."

"Sharp thinking." Her glove was on my cheek. Then she took it away, to light a cigarette. "It's the future all the same. Depends on if you're coming or going. Like I said, you're coming back. Anyway, what we've got here is the ultrafuture, baby. And what you've got now is what they call a prelude. Sweet things, preludes."

"What are we watching below?"

"That's the pageant under one of the unbridges."

The next night we were on a marvellous carousel of blue and gold and white, the turning horses rising and falling on their poles. Over the zephyrs of fairground organ music that seemed to buffet us soft-and-swiftly along as if each horse were a Pegasus, I called out:

"Will you tell me about the unbridges?"

I had been very concerned about them.

"Well," said Lara, her voice perfectly audible, as if coated in nail polish and shielded from interference, "that's all to do with the gods and the idols. This is the way is was told me: First, you didn't really have to go anywhere. There was a bridge, but no one was crossing it. You just had to be on it, watching the water run underneath. Then people started crossing the bridge. But the more they crossed it, the longer it got. Then it turned into the unbridge, 'cause no one could ever cross it. So it was kind of like being back at the beginning in a way, except that now there were two sides of the river, and everything existed between, and it was the most beautiful and amazing thing ever, except for the fact it was completely nowhere."

When we descended from the horses, we wandered through a strange fairground with an ambiance of endlessness about the cuckoo-clock details of each stall, ride and little quaintness we stopped at. I think we wandered right through from one night's dream to the next, though I am not sure exactly where the boundary or turnstile might have been.

We walked through an orchard where blue apples fell into our palms, as if time were reversed and, played in proper sequence, would show the apples rising from our palms to the trees. When we tired of this game, we found a place among the trees where blue blossoms fell, and here Lara laid out a blanket and arranged a picnic on it, with a round, blue cake at the centre. We contemplated the cake for some time. The letters O-M-G were written in the frosting on its upper surface, as if engraved on a tablet.

"How do we cut the cake without a knife?" she asked.

This precipitated in me a fidgety panic, and I searched myself for a many-bladed pocket knife.

"The perfect lock has no key," she said. "Do you know what 'OMG' is?"

"No," I said.

"It's Omega without the vowels."

"…Oh. But there is a vowel."

"That's not a vowel. This is what we call the technology of perfection, see? This cake is perfect."

And she waved her hand over the cake as if casting a spell on it.

"You have to put last things first," she said, looking me in the eye as if giving me the cake's secret recipe. "This cake exists because it's perfect. It was perfect before it existed. That's how you designed the ultravulva. That's how the ultrafuture will redesign you. See? Even though you're not here yet, I'm waiting. We both are. And then… we'll have the cake here, and eat it."

"You mean… eat it and have it?"

"That too," she said, and smiled, but there was a flicker of trouble or pity in her smile, and I felt myself receding from her, as if someone were pulling the picnic blanket with only me on it, away from her.

Blossoms whirled and seemed to fall on a bubble-gilded and glissando-rippling surface of water that now divided us. Perhaps I was drowning; perhaps she was. I had to tell myself to have faith in two contradictory things: that it was a dream, and that it was real.

There is one more of these instruction-tryst dreams I want to note. The dreams had been getting more and more blue, and one night I was in a room like that of the first dream, but entirely blue instead of red. It was different in other ways, too, being filled with enormous blue flowers, and even with some fauna to match this flora. But perhaps the most notable difference was that, before I materialised in the room, I seemed to see with unborn senses how that room was located within the ultravulva. I was zooming in on it the way I had when drawing higher magnifications of the supreme genitalia, only now I was zooming in from all directions, seeing the room as a multifaceted jewel chamber, suspended in the complex foil of living ornamentation. This, Lara told me (as usual, she awaited my arrival), was the Little Blue Ballroom. Here, she said, we would not talk as before; here we would dance. And so we did.

It was an unconfirmed feeling, and therefore uncertain, but it grew in confidence—we did not now need to talk, and lack of speech here implied no rebuff. Things were being communicated in a weave of motions and in pulses of sensation that seemed virtually telepathic. It is in the nature of those things that I cannot verbalise them. I feel my lack of time now, in writing this. If time is cloth, I don't have enough of it left to cover the body of my story, but will have to do my best to be an ingenious tailor and make the cutting short seem neat. For a start, I can dispense with describing indescribable feelings. I can skip straight to some of the results of those feelings. As I danced with Lara, certain things became clear that it seems I was meant to understand. Firstly, there was more than one Lara; reeling round the dance floor, I passed from one Lara to another a number of times before I realised what was happening. Perhaps there were also many of me, partnering the many Laras—I could not be sure. But of course there are many Laras, I thought; she is in motion, and therefore many. And I saw then the figures of our dance as the different figures in a zooprax-iscope—moving because many. They were, indisputably, different figures. I had, myself, drawn many Laras, and how could I ever say the picture I drew on Wednesday was the same entity as that I drew on Sunday? And yet, it was. The nape of a neck, the line of a nose, the relation of eyes to mouth, a familiar quarter-profile. What made these images one though they were separate?

As we continued to dance, as if I were back in the first dream, with the red room, I forgot who it was I danced with. Surely the face was a little different to a minute ago, I thought. The eyes seemed a little paler, the lips as if crossed out. Then she twirled beneath my arm, turning away and back to face me, and I was more certain than ever—as if in reaction to my giddy doubt—that this was the same girl, the right girl, the one I had been dancing with from the start, if only I could remember her name, the one whose picture I had drawn at the beginning. Yes. It was my dear Jenny Mills.

My delight at this was so much like alarm that it apparently jarred me awake. I opened my eyes to a dark, pre-dawn room. For a while I lay in tremendous vacancy. Then I felt a smile form beneath my nose.

"Yes, Jenny," I said in my heart, "I am a man with dreams."

When I finally drew back the curtains, I saw the snow was beginning to thaw, but I was ready for this.

Just before the dreams started, I was called again to the Basil Wolverton Institute. There is something strange about that place. They have sea monkeys as menial staff there; something I have only seen before at Sea Monkey Kingdom.

I was informed, in the same room, smelling of dust and chemicals, where I had previously undertaken various tests, that a new batch of volunteers would soon be required. It was not too late to opt out, they said; don't answer now, think about it for a day or two (no longer), then answer.

I saw the sea monkey mopping the floor in the corridor as I was leaving, and I made up my mind. My mind was made up, but I still had not finishing agonising. The next day I gave my reply—I was ready.

That was six weeks ago.

Blue on blue—like losing oneself in the layers of a summer sky. There may be something outside the sky, but the sky itself never ends. The summer passes, but the summer sky is endless; the autumn passes, but the autumn night is endless. And winter, when blue deepens to black, seems like it will never pass, but it does, back to spring again, and the beginning, although it is a different beginning than you knew before. As in the song, the blue of spring is the oldest, yet the latest thing. The original,

and yet the strangest thing. It has never seemed stranger
to me than now.

I had somehow, tenuously, layer upon layer, blue
upon blue, been anticipating this very combination of
things, my stomach tickling delicately with the unbearable, precarious hugeness of it, as, little by little, things
progressed.

I believe I know what teleportation can do to a living
being. I know. I believe I have seen the reality, or part of
it. In fact, this helps.

A year ago, when I was more the kind of man to
speak impulsively—even angrily—about dreams, to attractive women I hardly knew, I probably thought I had
faith in the imagination. Now I have agreed to step inside
the teleportation chamber. The one certainty is that the
person writing these words will be vaporised. It is what
comes next that is uncertain. Imagination is nothing—
just children's games. I cannot control my terror. And
yet, even within this terror, I control myself and find
strange points of comfort, of blossoming tranquillity.

I keep thinking, for instance, of my signature on that
waiver. My participation in the experiment is official. It's
in black and white. Why is this reassuring? Funeral rites
are also a kind of formality, but they don't bring a person
back to life. And yet, even knowing that it's absurd—or
because it is—the fact that I have been officially told that
there is nothing to fear comforts me. If I am vaporised,
I will be, in some sense, officially vaporised, which fact
has an entirely different metaphysical status than some
haphazard or malign vaporisation.

But I mention this really as a way of explaining something more important. I only begin to understand what faith might mean now that I am terrified. I tried to pray, but it seemed too impersonal and meaningless. And then, with the instinct of desperation, I thought of Lara. It is to Lara I pray. A chasm is between us, and in that chasm I do not—cannot—exist. But on the other side of it is Lara. And what is Lara? A pansy-sweet, fictional pin-up—the kind of pin-up I should even be a little embarrassed to have on my wall, at once a little too strumpety cheap and a little too squishily personal. Yes, this is madness. Worse—it's pathetic. I tried again to think of some sober, lofty, universal power, to which I might appeal. It was no good. It had to be Lara, and I turned to her again as if I had been long restrained and could stand it no more.

Yes, let it be Lara. Laugh at me—I may or may not laugh along. Anyway, I don't care. On the other side of that chasm is Lara. Nothing else matters.

V: Coda

THOUGH he has gone, Victor Sernik Winton is still one of the best artists I've worked with. Sure, he had his limitations, but it seems to me Victor's problem was this: he was always pushing against those limitations. Because he focused on them so much, they were more visible to his readers, whereas all he had accomplished and should have been patting himself on the back for—which, I think, was a lot more than most comic book illustrators—became invisible, or nearly—a kind of secret treasure.

Victor died, or should I say, disappeared, in the year 1958i (ASAF), April the 9th. He was thirty-seven years old. In the previous year I had commissioned from him a story called *Lara Strikes it Lucky*, featuring his latest character creation, Lara Lovelily. I thought this could make a good series. It wasn't too clear who the audience for the strip was, but it had something that you might call pizzazz. Who knows what would have happened if Victor had lived longer? Maybe he wouldn't have made a big name for himself, but I'm sure he still hadn't quite hit his stride, and he had at least another ten years of quality creative work in him. If nothing else, if he'd lived there would be a little more colour and pizzazz to go round in this world.

This isn't an obituary, but before I cut to the chase, I would like to make this one small tribute to Victor: his drawing could be a little idiosyncratic, and sometimes I got the feeling that somewhere one or another of his stories just didn't make sense. But in the middle of a busy week of editing, getting back hackwork that had been rushed for a deadline, or perfectly good work from someone who was just waiting to do something better with his life, or, worse sometimes, from someone who already fit right in, any time I got new work from Victor, it wasn't business as usual. My mood would always change when I read one of Victor's. I'd close the office door, put my feet up, and take a little time. Victor wasn't always credited for his work, but whenever *I* ran something of his, I made sure he got credited. I hope he goes on getting more and more credit.

But Victor's name will live on in another way. In a plaque on the wall of the Basil Wolverton Institute, separate to the plaque provided for the other teleportation volunteers, the following memorial may be read:

> In Memory of Victor Sernik Winton, who
> dematerialised one afternoon in April and
> never rematerialised. Because of this loss,
> we make sure today to keep all data safe.

The technicians running the project were sure there would be no insurmountable problems. Even if the data that made a person was reassembled incorrectly at the other end of a teleport transmission, as long as the data itself was retained, in theory nothing was lost. They could destroy the faulty copy if necessary (just as the original had been destroyed) and try again indefinitely. No one anticipated what happened with Victor. The original Victor vanished after his data was read, then a transmission was made, but nothing was received at the other terminal. They checked all their settings and tried again, but not only had Victor gone, his data was also nowhere. It had evaporated. There's some technical explanation as to why—something to do with 'transposition intervals,' whatever they are. This is not the place for a lengthy treatment of the reasons behind this misfortune, but it seems that because humans are complex objects configured in their most important details from the influences of both nature and nurture, these 'transposition intervals' are necessary for storing their data in a 'live' rather than 'inert' state. What is stored is a kind of superposition, and the method of writing this kind of data is called 'hydragraphology.' In layman's terms, the data cannot remain in one place, but must be juggled. Somewhere along the line, in Victor's case, the machine dropped the balls and lost everything that Victor Winton ever was. That's all fixed, they say, for *future* teleporters (although now, of course, Dr. Ingram's big battle is with the Temporal Planning Permission Committee), and when the hundreds of test subjects have gone back to their regular lives and lived a bit, maybe people will be ready in general for teleportation. For now, of course, it's military use only.

You might think that I'm writing this only to make the bizarre end to Victor's life a little better known, but for me there's something else that is not only more bizarre but more important. I know well enough that plenty of people who read this won't find anything of particular significance in what comes next. It may be partly because I was the first person to piece it together—or think I was—and partly because I knew Victor, but I do find it significant. I would guess that if you needed me to explain why then there'd be no point in trying to explain.

Victor left his unpublished work to me. It seems like he didn't entirely believe the assurances of safety that he had been given about teleportation; he'd drawn up a rudimentary will near the end. A sealed envelope addressed to me contained the manuscript reproduced in the pages preceding this coda. There was a note attached to the manuscript with a paperclip. It said:

> Dear Mr. Farnley,
>
> Enclosed is the only sequel I can provide to *Lara Strikes It Lucky*. I'm not sure you'll find a place for it this time, but I think I can truthfully say that it is the best I can do.
>
> Yours,
>
> Victor W.

Reading first the note, then the manuscript, I felt my mind being burglarised by new ideas and conjectures, long-shut drawers and closets being opened and their contents strewn wildly across the floor. This is a single example of the questions that disturbed me: If Victor—his copy, I mean—had materialised in the arrival terminal of the teleport circuit, what would he have thought of the manuscript he had left in that envelope when he returned to his daily life?

Victor was right. It wasn't easy to place the story as a sequel to *Lara Strikes It Lucky*, and for a long while I kept it to myself—going through its pages again sometimes—wondering if there might even be a sequel to this sequel, or at least an epilogue. One result of this was that I got hold of the two volumes of *Magic Daoism* that Victor seemed to put such faith in, and read them for myself. I was surprised when, a couple of years ago, a third volume was published. I hadn't even been convinced the author or authors was or were still alive, and nothing in the publicity of the books explained their origins. Interested readers should investigate for themselves, of course, if they find copies that have survived the patchy and inexplicable ban.

Something I read in that third volume eventually tipped the scales in my mind in favour of publishing *Blue on Blue*, and that is why you now hold in your hands this special edition of *Future Marvels*. It's too much a convention of weird and science fiction tales now to say "the following is a true story." I will not make such a statement here. I believe it is unnecessary to protest the truth in such a case. I must have the same kind of faith that Victor had in Lara—that the truth will reveal and hide itself as necessary.

All that's left now is one excerpt from *Magic Daoism, Volume III*. The passage in question is a description of a scene from an unknown television show. The author claims that the show is a broadcast from the future:

> The broadcast, which was scheduled on no listed timetable, began abruptly, without introduction, and I would have been sure that I was seeing something from halfway through, if not for some indefinable atmosphere of awakening in the scene that subtly convinced me this was as much from the start as anything gets.
>
> There was a grove of trees on a wooded eminence, and a man was sitting upon a white horse, while one of the trees blazed with flames nearby. The horse was standing placidly, as if it had stood thus for some time. This scene continued for a number of minutes. It was much longer than is normally allowed for a scene without action or dialogue, and seemed to be happening in the same current of time as my own breathing. Nor did it induce the boredom that a poorly edited film sometimes does. If the man was acting, he was surely a genius to bring the passing moments so much to life.

Eventually, some noise from among the trees heralded the arrival of a young red-headed woman in a yellow dress. It was hard to tell if the man recognised her or not, but he responded readily enough to her presence, dismounting from the horse at her bidding and with her help, and following her through the trees. The colours of the scene had a more-than-real quality to them, as if tinted in some way, creating a fragrant sense of both freshness and age, mellowness and bright charm. The many branches were rich with fruit and flowers. As they walked, taking a slender, winding, downward path, they made conversation, something like this:

"That was lucky."

"It's only lucky if it might not have happened."

"I think, maybe it might not have."

"If it's happened, how can you say it might not have?"

"Because… because it was lucky."

"Maybe it can be lucky anyway, even if it was bound to happen."

"You're changing your mind now."

"I know."

"I agree—either way, it was lucky."

There was also some talk of the horse, and of where the path led. The woman looked back sometimes at the man. He looked at her, but also continued to gaze about himself in rapture. There was something indescribably unusual about the woman's appearance. I wondered if perhaps, for some reason, she was being played by more than one actress, but there was never anything obvious that enabled me to answer this question with certainty. The man, anyway, if he noticed anything unusual about her, was either indifferent to it, or was positively enlivened by it.

He chuckled to himself sometimes, and there was such a quality to his laugh that I found myself intensely concerned as to what it might mean. Was this because of the girl and her friendly face that was inexplicably the same and inexplicably changeful from moment to moment? Then the girl spoke and my attention was brought to heightened focus.

"Watcha laughin' at?" she asked over her shoulder, half laughing herself.

"I can't work it out—everything is more like the first time than ever before, but... if that were true, there shouldn't be an 'ever before.' But there is an ever before."

"Sure there is. It just hasn't happened yet."

They came to a clearing, in which was a wooden ranch-like building. Stopping at the threshold of the front door, they embraced spontaneously, then entered. The rooms were full of the same strange-familiar colours as the woods through which they'd passed, with framed photographs, a patterned tablecloth and a fireplace giving the brightness and richness that in the woods had been provided by fruit and flowers.

The man sighed as if something overflowed him.

The woman turned again at this sound.

She smiled her enquiry.

"Can I just look at you a moment?" he asked.

Though she said nothing and did not move, she seemed to say, with gentle gravity, yes.

"Nothing's going to be lost for long," she said, after the moment seemed naturally to have passed. "Do you believe me?"

He nodded. There was uncertainty in it, shading, it seemed, at the end to certainty. Both seeing and feeling this at once, they smiled and gasped in unison.

"Then what shall we do?" he asked.

"First, rest. Then… everything you remember. This place is just a home from home. We can walk to the blue valley, and then… wait, there's something I've got to show you."

She took him by the elbow and led him into the next room.

For a moment, on the right, the camera—if it was a camera—disclosed something wondrous. It appeared an aquarium had been built into that wall, but among the coral, sea-weed and colonies of sea anemones, most of the space was taken up by a fantastical castle about whose minarets and turrets played a strange glittering, as if there might be such a thing as underwater fireworks. Moreover, this castle was inhabited. A traveller in the wilderness deprived of human company for months might feel excited at the prospect of entering a city and knowing again the stir of intelligence. This castle and its watery environs also flickered with intelligence such as would be balm and restorative to the weary soul, but it was not human intelligence.

There was only the briefest glimpse of this, however, then the view moved to the colours the aquarium threw on the floor, as from some submarine stained-glass window, and then I saw what the woman was showing the man.

A window was framed as squarely and prettily in the far wall as a painting. But this painting stirred in a breeze that trembled as with joy.

She pointed, satisfied, and turned her

eyes to his in accomplished understanding.

"The second time is the real first time," she said. "Outside is inside now. We have our own land and the branch blossoms outside the window."

They turned to look at the window again together. Snow was falling now, and it was dark.

"See?" said the woman.

A blizzard filled the camera and the broadcast ended.

For more context, I recommend the interested reader investigate the three volumes of *Magic Daoism*.

I have one last thing to note. Victor did not stop writing after he finished the manuscript he left to me. Some notes in his handwriting appear to have been worked on in his final days. These are very fragmentary and hard to decipher, but, in their concentration on the single concern of the sea monkeys, are suggestive. Victor describes sea monkeys as "multi-dimensionally amphibious." It could be that questions regarding the sea monkeys were among the last things on Victor's mind, but if so there is no coherent conclusion to be derived from the notes. I only want to quote here what Victor lists as the four meanings of snow in sea monkey culture. How he came by this information I have no idea, but it seems to provide a further clue in what I believe is a genuine mystery. Others, no doubt, will think I am seeing patterns in bladderwrack by moonlight.

The four meanings of snow:

1. Death, of course.
2. Borders of things, and what is in between. In this sense, the static between radio stations is also snow.
3. Disintegration. Rearrangement. Complete loss of form.
4. The most intimate meeting.

J. Farnley, 1954j (ASAF)

The Cover Artist

IT WON'T take you long to conclude that she's not your usual pin-up. There's no preening, no silly posing or tripping over her drawers. She's not even looking at you. For a pin-up she seems oddly dignified. Her self-possession evokes a very modern sensibility, yet there's also a timeless quality about her. But don't confuse it with retro; there are none of the clichéd props or costumes artists fall back on to force the impression of nostalgia into their work. You may be surprised to learn she was painted nearly eighty years ago for an obscure pulp called *Spicy Stories*. The magazine was so scandalous that the day it was printed police would yank it off the magazine rack and, for good measure, toss the newsstand vendor in the slammer.

The artist responsible for this now not so controversial figure is Enoch Bolles. Born in 1883, Bolles trained at the National Academy of Design and the Art Students League, two of the leading educational institutions for commercial artists. His first covers appeared on the stands in the 1910s, the very time when colour illustration came into wide use in magazines. A favourite among readers, his work for the magazine *Judge* was reprinted and sold as posters. In 1923 Bolles was hired to be the cover artist for the movie humour magazine *Film Fun*, a monthly periodical light on stories but heavy on glamour photos of starlets. Over the next two decades he painted virtually every cover, over 200 in all, as well as another 400 or so for a score of other titles. Between magazine assignments Bolles completed scores of illustrations, all lavishly rendered in oil, for products ranging from cigarettes to hosiery, making him one of the most prolific commercial artists of his time. But in the late 1930s his career was stalled by psychological problems that required hospital visits and in 1943 it was over, the consequence of a shrinking market and his worsening condition. Institutionalised for the next three decades, Bolles continued to paint, for pleasure in addition to producing commissioned portraits. Throughout it all he maintained close touch with his large family through letters and hospital visits (hardly the portrait of a raving maniac). Bolles left the hospital for good in 1969 and returned to the house where he had raised his family. He died in 1976 at the age of ninety-three.

The career of Enoch Bolles bookended the entirety of the Golden Era of Illustration, a period when the popularity of the leading magazine illustrators rivalled the movie stars they painted. Among the most prolific and visible of all magazine artists, Bolles laboured in what may have been a self-enforced anonymity. No longer.

Today he is widely acclaimed as one of a small cadre of artists who established the tone and form of the modern pin-up, and his work continues to exert considerable influence. Yet despite over a decade of personal research on Bolles, he remains, to me, a stubbornly enigmatic figure. And so it shouldn't be a surprise about that girl on the cover; the closer you try to get, the more distant and inaccessible she becomes.

—Jack Raglin